6/18

T-10

2016-9

L 11/16

6-20(15)

THE KERRIGANS

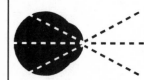

THE KERRIGANS

A TEXAS DYNASTY

WILLIAM W. JOHNSTONE
WITH J.A. JOHNSTONE

WHEELER PUBLISHING
A part of Gale, Cengage Learning

GALE
CENGAGE Learning·

Farmington Hills, Mich • San Francisco • New York • Waterville, Maine
Meriden, Conn • Mason, Ohio • Chicago

GALE
CENGAGE Learning®

Copyright © 2014 by J. A. Johnstone.
Wheeler Publishing, a part of Gale, Cengage Learning.

ALL RIGHTS RESERVED
Following the death of William W. Johnstone, the Johnstone family is working with a carefully selected writer to organize and complete Mr. Johnstone's outlines and many unfinished manuscripts to create additional novels in all of his series like The Last Gunfighter, Mountain Man, and Eagles, among others. This novel was inspired by Mr. Johnstone's superb storytelling.
The WWJ steer head logo is a trademark of Kensington Publishing Corp.
Wheeler Publishing Large Print Western.
The text of this Large Print edition is unabridged.
Other aspects of the book may vary from the original edition.
Set in 16 pt. Plantin.

LIBRARY OF CONGRESS CATALOGING-IN-PUBLICATION DATA

Johnstone, William.
  The Kerrigans : a Texas dynasty / William Johnstone with J.A. Johnstone.
    pages cm. — (Wheeler Publishing large print western)
    ISBN 978-1-4104-8370-6 (paperback) — ISBN 1-4104-8370-3 (softcover)
    1. Large type books. I. Johnstone, J. A. II. Title.
PS3560.O415K47 2015
813'.54—dc23   2015029671

Published in 2015 by arrangement with Pinnacle Books, an imprint of Kensington Publishing Corp.

Printed in the United States of America
1 2 3 4 5 6 7 19 18 17 16 15

THE KERRIGANS

CHAPTER ONE

"You had to do it, Miz Kerrigan," Sheriff Miles Martin said, hat in hand. "He came looking for trouble."

Kate Kerrigan stood at her parlor window, stared into moon-dappled darkness, and said nothing.

"I mean, he planned to rob you, and after you fed him, an' all," Martin said.

Kate turned, a tall, elegant woman. Her once flaming red hair was now gray but her fine-boned, Celtic beauty was still enough to turn a man's head.

She smiled at Martin.

"He planned to murder me, Miles. Cover his tracks, I guess."

"Where is Trace?" Martin said.

"Out on the range, and so is his brother," Kate said.

"And Miss Ivy and Miss Shannon?"

"My segundo's wife is birthing a child. Doc Woodruff is off fly-fishing somewhere, so Ivy and Shannon went over to Lucy Cobb's cabin to help. Lucy has already had three, so I don't foresee any problems."

Then as though she feared she was tempting fate, Kate said in the lilting Irish brogue she'd never lost, "May Jesus, Mary, and Joseph and all the saints in heaven protect her this night."

"He was a city slicker," Martin said.

The sheriff, a drink of water with a walrus mustache and sad brown eyes, stood in front of the fire. He had a Colt self-cocker in his holster and a silver star pinned to the front of his sheepskin.

The fall of 1907 had been cold and the winter was shaping up to be a sight worse.

"He had the look of one," Kate said.

Martin looked uncomfortable and awkward, all big hands and spurred boots. He chose his words carefully, like a barefoot man walking through a nettle patch.

"How did it happen, Miz Kerrigan? I need to ask."

"Of course, Miles," Kate said. "Why don't you sit and I'll get you a brandy. Only to keep out the chill, you understand."

The big lawman sat gratefully in the studded, leather chair by the fire.

"I'm right partial to brandy," he said. "Warms a man's insides, I always say."

8

Kate poured brandy in two huge snifters, handed one to Martin and settled herself in the chair opposite.

The lawman thought she sat like a queen, and why not? Kate's range was larger than some European kingdoms.

Martin played for time.

He produced the makings and said, "May I beg your indulgence, Ma'am?"

"Please do. My son Quinn is much addicted to cigarettes, a habit he learned from our vaqueros who smoke like chimneys."

"Doctors say it's good for the chest," Martin said.

"So I've heard, but I do not set store by what doctors say."

Kate sipped her brandy, and then stooped to poke the logs into life. She didn't look up.

"I've killed men before, Miles."

"I know, Miz Kerrigan, but I was trying to spare you a lot of fool questions."

The woman's emerald green eyes fixed on Martin's face.

"I'll tell you what happened here earlier this evening and you can ask your questions as you see fit."

The lawman nodded.

"I'd given the servants the night off, and I was alone in the house when I heard a horse

9

come to a halt outside."

"What time was that, Miz Kerrigan?"

"It was seven o'clock. I was here, sitting by the fire eating the cold supper the cook had prepared for me, and heard the grandfather clock chime in the hallway. A few moments later a knock came to the door."

Kate's blue silk day dress rustled as she sat back and made herself more comfortable.

"I answered the summons and opened to a man, an ordinary looking fellow wearing an old dark jacket that was several sizes too large for him. He had no overcoat; the evening was cold and he shivered.

"He said he was hungry and could I spare him a bite of food? Since I'd no kitchen staff available, I opened the door and let him come inside."

"That was a mistake, Miz Kerrigan," Martin said.

Kate smiled.

"Miles, over the years I've let many men into this house. Geronimo once sat where you're sitting. We had tea and cake and he wanted to talk about old Queen Vic."

The lawman stirred uncomfortably in his chair and glanced over his shoulder, as though he expected to see the old Apache's ghost glowering at him from a corner.

"Well, I led the way to the kitchen and the man followed me. He said his name was Tom and that he was looking for ranch work. He had the most singular eyes, rather mean and foxy, like those I used to see in some Texas gunmen back in the old days. I must admit, I did not trust him."

"You did right," Martin said. "Not trusting him, I mean."

"Thank you, Miles. I'm sure your approval will stand me in good stead should you consider hanging me."

"Miz Kerrigan! I have no intention . . . I mean . . . I wouldn't . . ."

Kate gave the flustered lawman a dazzling smile.

"There, there, Miles, don't distress yourself. I'm certain the facts of the case will speak for themselves and banish all doubt from your mind."

"Yes, yes, I'm sorry. Please proceed."

Martin was fifty years old and Kate Kerrigan could still make him blush.

"I fixed the man some beef sandwiches, and indeed, he was as wolf hungry as he professed," Kate said. "It was after he'd eaten heartily that things took a dangerous turn."

"Was the sugar scattered all over the kitchen floor part of it?" Martin said.

"Indeed it was. A small sugar sack had been left on the counter by a careless maid and Tom, if that was really his name —"

"It wasn't," Martin said.

Kate looked at him in surprise.

"Please go on, Miz Kerrigan," the lawman said.

"Well, the man jumped up, grabbed the sugar sack and threw the contents over the floor. He shoved the empty sack at me and said, 'You, fill this. The jewels you're wearing first.'"

"'Mister,'" I said, "'I've been threatened by more dangerous bad men than you.'"

Martin reached into the pocket of his coat and withdrew a revolver.

"Then he drew this on you."

Kate glanced at the gun.

"Yes, that's it, a Hopkins and Allen in thirty-two caliber. He said to fill the sack or he'd scatter my brains."

"Oh, Miz Kerrigan, you must have been terrified," Martin said.

Kate shook her head.

"Miles, you've known me how long? Thirty years? You should remember by now I don't scare easily." She frowned. "And for God's sake, call me Kate. You never called me anything else until I got this big house and eight hundred thousand acres of range to go with it."

Now it was the lawman's turn to smile.

"Kate it is, and you're right, you never did scare worth a damn, beggin' your pardon."

"I also used to cuss, Miles, before I became a lady."

"You were always a lady, Kate. Even when all you had to your name was a cabin and a milk cow and a passel of young 'uns."

Kate nodded.

"Hard times in Texas back in those days after the war."

"We'll wind it up," Martin said. "It's growing late and I'm only going through the motions anyhow."

"The fact remains that I killed a man tonight, Miles. It's your duty to hear me out."

Kate rose, poured more brandy from the decanter into the lawman's glass and then her own.

She sat by the fire again and said, "When the man pointed the gun at me, I took off my necklace and bracelets and dropped them in the sack. He wanted my wedding ring, but I refused. When he looked at it and saw it was but a cheap silver band, he demanded the expensive stuff.

"I told him I kept my jewelry in my bedroom and he told me to take him there.

He also made an extremely crude suggestion and vowed he'd have his way with me."

"The damned rogue," Martin said, his mustache bristling.

"In my day I've heard worse than that, but right then I knew I was in real danger."

Kate's elegant fingers strayed to the simple cross that now hung around her neck.

"There's not much left to tell, Miles. I played the petrified, hysterical matron to perfection and when we went upstairs I told the robber that my jewels were in my dresser drawer."

Kate smiled.

"How often men are undone by their lusts. The wretch was so intent on unbuttoning the back of my dress that he didn't see me reach into the dresser drawer and produce — not diamonds — but my old Colt forty-four."

"Bravo!" Martin said, lifting his booted feet off the rug and clicking his heels.

"I wrenched away from him, leveled my revolver and ordered him to drop his gun. His face twisted into a most demonic mask and he cursed and raised his gun."

"The murderous rogue!" Martin said.

"I fired," Kate said. "John Wesley Hardin once told me to belly shoot a man and I'd drop him in his tracks. I followed Wes's advice — the only bit of good advice he ever gave me or mine — and hit the bandit where a respectable man's watch fob would have been."

"But he got off a shot," Martin said. He reached into his pocket again and held up the spent .32. "Dug it out of your bedroom wall."

"Yes, he got off a shot but he was already a dead man. He dropped to the floor, groaned for a few moments and then all the life in him left."

"Kate, you've been through a terrible ordeal," Martin said.

"I've been through it before, Miles. The man who came here was intent on raping and robbing me. I fight to keep what is mine, whether it's a diamond ring or a single head of cattle. I've hanged rustlers and other men who would threaten *Ciaro-gan* and as God as my witness I'll do it again if I have to."

Sheriff Martin's eyes revealed that he believed every word Kate had just said.

He'd known some tough, fighting ranchers, but none even came close to Kate Kerrigan's grit and determination.

She'd built an empire, then held it against all comers, an amazon in petticoats.

Martin built a cigarette and without looking up from the makings, he spoke.

"His name was Frank Ross. He'd served five years of a life sentence in Huntsville for murder and rape when he killed a guard and escaped. He later murdered a farmer and his wife near Leesville and stole three dollars and a horse."

Martin lit his cigarette.

"Then he came here."

"Miles, why didn't you tell me all this before?" Kate said.

"After what you've gone through, I didn't want to alarm you."

Martin read the question on the woman's face and shrank from the green fire in her eyes. She had an Irish temper, did Kate Kerrigan, and the sheriff wanted no part of it.

"I got a wire a couple of days ago from the Leesburg marshal and he warned that Ross could come this way," he said. "I never thought it could happen the way it did."

"It did happen," Kate said.

"Yes, Kate, I know, and I'm sorry."

Martin rose to his feet.

"I'll be going now. One of my deputies took the body away. You should know that. I'll see myself out."

The big lawman stepped to the door, his spurs chiming.

He stopped and said, "My respects to your fine family."

"And mine to Mrs. Martin."

Martin nodded.

"I'll be sure to tell her that."

Kate Kerrigan had defended herself and her honor, just another battle to stand alongside all the others that had gone before.

But the killing of Frank Ross hung heavy on her, and she felt the need for closeness, to hold something her husband, dead so many years, had touched.

All she had was the ring on her finger . . . and the letter that had begun it all.

Kate walked to her office, unlocked the writing bureau, and took the worn, yellowed scrap of paper from a drawer.

She returned to the parlor, poured herself brandy, and sat again by the ashy fire.

After a while, she opened the letter and read it again for perhaps the thousandth time . . . the letter that had founded a dynasty.

CHAPTER TWO

In April 1862, on the eve of a battle that would pass into American legend, a barefoot Johnny Reb handed a sealed letter to another.

"You'll give it to her, Michael, give it into the hand of my Kate," Joseph Kerrigan of Ireland's green and fair County Sligo said.

"And why would I, Joseph Kerrigan?" Michael Feeny said. "When you'll be able enough to give it to her yourself."

Kerrigan, a handsome young man with eyes the color of a Donegal mist, shook his head.

"That I will not," he said. "Did you not hear it yourself in the night, out there among the pines?"

"Hear what?" Feeny said, his puzzled face freckled all over like a sparrow's egg.

"The banshee, Michael. She screamed my name. Over and over again, coming from her skull mouth, my name . . . my name . . ."

"Jesus, Mary, and Joseph and Saints Peter and Paul, it cannot be so, Joseph. You heard the wind in the trees, only the wind."

"You'll give my Katherine the letter," Kerrigan said. "She's a strong woman and after she reads it she'll know what to do. And tell her this also, that her husband fell fighting for a noble cause and brought no disgrace to his name."

"And it's an ancient and honorable name you bear, Joseph Kerrigan, to be sure," Feeny said. "You say you heard the banshee, and I will not call you a liar, but she screams for someone else, not you. Many men will die this day and the next."

"And I will number among them," Kerrigan said.

He shoved the folded letter into Feeny's hands.

"As you see it is sealed, Michael. Captain O'Neil used his own candle and impressed the molten wax with the signet off his finger. And why not, since I have no ring of my own and the captain's bears the crest of Irish kings?"

The two young soldiers marched together, the swaying, shambling, distance-eating tramp of the Confederate infantry.

Their regiment, the 52nd Tennessee, was part of Braxton Bragg's Second Corps of

19

the Army of the Mississippi, and there wasn't a man who shouldered a rifle that day who didn't believe that he could take on the entire Yankee army by himself and send them running all the way across the Potomac.

"I'm charging you with a great duty, Michael," Kerrigan said. "Contained in that letter you bear so carelessly tells Katherine what she and our children must do to go on without me, and, if need be, where she can find help to do it."

Michael Feeny thrust the letter back toward Kerrigan.

"No need for it," he said. "Give it to her from your own hand when all this is done."

"When all this is done, I will be done as well," Kerrigan said. "Think you, Michael, that the banshee cries for no reason?"

"A man knows not the hour of his death, Joseph. If he could, what man would walk blindly into the path of a galloping carriage or cross a railroad track at the wrong moment?"

Feeny doffed his kepi and wiped sweat from his brow with the back of his hand.

"The banshee is a demon, but God is with us, Joseph. Ah man, you will bear whatever message you have to your Katherine upon your own lips."

"It will not be, Michael. I have no desire to die on the field of honor, but I am confident that is my fate. But even so, I hope so very powerfully that I am wrong and you are right. Death is no boon companion whose company I seek."

Feeny grinned, and placed the kepi at a jaunty angle back on his head.

"Remember this one?" he said.

He tilted back his head and sang.

"Oh, my name is George Campbell
and at the age of eighteen
I fought for old Erin her rights to maintain,
And many a battle did I undergo,
Commanded by that hero called General
      Munroe."

A big, grizzled soldier with corporal's stripes tapped Feeny on the shoulder and grinned.

"And didn't we English stick his honor's head on a pike at Lisburn castle?"

"Aye you did, and be damned to ye," Feeny said. "You should be marching for the Tyrant, Englishman, and not for the South."

The big man laughed and said no more.

"Well, that's taken the song from my lips," Feeny said. "Let us then keep hope before us instead. Make no prediction of your own doom, Joseph. Walk bold and tall into whatever soldier's hell is ahead for us, and come out alive on the other end. Perhaps both of us will come out together."

"Aye, perhaps. But I cannot presume upon providence when my conviction is so strong. So I ask you to bear this letter on your body through the fight ahead. I have another copy of the same inside my own jacket, in case you should be taken away in battle along with me. Sometimes those letters are found and sent on to the families after the dead are carried from the field."

"All this woeful talk falls far shy of prudence, Joseph Kerrigan. My sainted old grandmother told me that the things we speak go to God's ear, and He sometimes causes them to come to pass. So talk of life, not death."

"Very well. If God is kind to both of us, we will rejoice. But if I should die and you live, then I ask you to go, as first opportunity allows, to Nashville and present it to my beloved and tell her my spirit will watch over her all her days. I don't trust the army to get the letter to her. You, I do trust."

Feeny was ready to argue further with Kerrigan. He did not, though, instead merely laying his hand briefly on the other's shoulder. "I give you my promise, good Joe. I expect never to be called on to fulfill it, but if fate brings ill to you and I survive, I pledge to you that your wife will receive from my own hand what you've given me. I vow it on the grave of my sainted mother."

Kerrigan turned to his companion, shifting his rifle sling as he did so.

"Your mother is alive and well, Mike."

"And so she is, hale and hearty and as fond of the gin as ever. But her grave, or the place it will be, exists somewhere, empty for now, and it is that grave on which I vowed."

"You are an odd old crow, Mike. An odd crow, or the devil take me."

"I am odd, and know it. But also trustworthy. You can count on me to carry that letter to Nashville if it falls to me to do it."

"I know it will not be easy, my friend. The federals took Nashville in February. Travel in these times is no Sunday stroll."

"Aye. Even so, Joe. Even so."

Joseph Kerrigan nodded and blinked fast, hard-fought emotion struggling inside him. He managed to choke it back and respond with a simple: "Thank you, Mike."

"Think nothing of it. There will be nothing for me to do, because we will live through this fight, you and I. Let me hear you say it, Joseph."

"We will . . . will live through this fight. Both of us."

"Aye indeed, and come out the other end heroes, with a gold medal on our chests."

"That's how it will be, Michael, lay to that." But there was no conviction in Kerrigan's voice.

All Joseph Kerrigan would experience of the famed Battle of Shiloh, which commenced early the next morning, was a series of events that entered his consciousness in a troubling jumble, running together, bleeding one into the other in a welter of confusion it would require much time to untangle.

No such time would be given him.

In the brief period he had left to know anything at all, Joe Kerrigan would be immediately conscious of only a few things, beginning with the feeling of his own heart pounding as if trying to exit his chest when the call came from the orderly sergeant to check armaments and prepare to advance.

Kerrigan would be aware, in a distant, numbed way, of standing and advancing into a rising crackle and blast of rifle fire and artillery beyond the cannon-blasted forest ahead of him. The foe had awakened and was beginning to resist the advancing Bonnie Blue Flag.

Mike Feeny was still at Kerrigan's side, and said, "Joe, I'm going to make another vow to you. One day you and I will return to this very bit of woods and enjoy a picnic here with our wives and children. These are pretty woods, except for what is happening here. It would be an ideal place for children to play, don't you think?"

"It would, Mike, of a truth. But I will make no plans until I know if what the banshee fated for me is truth or deception."

"Live, my friend. Live. Let death take others, but us live."

They advanced, drawing closer to gunfire unseen but loudly heard ahead of them.

Even now Kerrigan could see nothing he could make sense of, though the sound of the fight heightened and the screams of dying men grew louder.

Then he heard a puzzling rustling and rattling in the trees, a repeated tick-tick-tick sound, followed by a shower of leaves and small twigs.

The ticking, like the sound of rain dripping from eaves after a summer thunderstorm, came from soft lead Minie balls striking trees, the clattering and crackling and downfall of greenery from bullets clipping branches and twigs, denuding trees already struggling to fight off the barrenness of the winter past and clothe themselves for spring.

A man walking to Kerrigan's left grunted and fell, blood streaming down the front of his leg, pouring from a fresh wound. A big grizzled Englishman, he collapsed, groaning, and made only one effort to rise. A second Minie ball caught him in the chest and sent him flat to the ground, a red rose blossoming in the middle of his butternut shirt.

"Holy Mother Mary bless us and save us!" Feeny said, horrified, as he watched the corporal fall.

Kerrigan glanced at Feeny as two other men near them dropped, one wounded in the shoulder, the other shot through the chest and dead.

"This is hot work, Michael," he said. "But such a fire cannot last for long."

But the hail of gunfire sheeting toward the advancing Confederate line increased.

The thumping of lead hitting trees and men was now so steady as to drown out the sound of twigs and branches being clipped, though they drifted to the ground in an unceasing shower.

A command from somewhere just behind the line then ordered the soldiers to take shelter from the fire.

"They're killing us, boys!" the officer yelled. "Down on your bellies."

Kerrigan recognized the fine Irish voice of Captain O'Neil, but it was hoarse and broken by shouting, inhuman stress and fear.

He, Feeny, and several others around them took cover behind the white, skeletal trunk of a fallen oak and there breathed the gasps of terrified men.

But at least they could still breathe, and for that Kerrigan voiced a silent prayer of thanks.

He turned on his back and reloaded his rifle; surprised the hand working powder, ball and ramrod was steady.

"This ain't really safe," said a deeply southern voice on the far side of Feeny. "This here log humps up on the bottom side so there's a space between it and the ground, see? Get down low enough and you can look right under. A bullet hits that gap and it's going to sail right through and —"

The man said no more.

His words about the protective deficiency of the warped log had been prophetic. He took a bullet through the face, its destructive course angling down from his forehead through sinuses and throat, lodging finally somewhere in his chest.

"Jesus, Mary, and Joseph," Feeny wailed. "Will you look at poor Anderson all shot through and through?"

He fingered a black rosary, blessed by a cardinal, and sounded like a man about to burst into tears.

"You were right, Joe . . . we will die here," he said.

Kerrigan's earlier morbid convictions about death had been all but forgotten after the first shots were fired.

He was scared, no question, but above and beyond that he was angry, filled with a biting fury at the very idea that men he did not know, and against whom he had done no violence, were trying to kill him.

A vision of his beautiful wife, Kate, rose in his mind and he vowed to her image that, dire premonitions be damned, he would fight to live, and return to her side.

Feeny, battling terror, proved that he had sand. And besides, as he was well aware, did not his name mean "brave soldier" in the ancient Gaelic?

He moved upward a little, leveled his rifle across the top of the log, and took aim in the general direction of the federals.

The action inspired Kerrigan to do the same, though neither of them had a precise target sighted.

Kerrigan defied fate and lifted his head above the protective height the log provided, readying to fire.

Then, in a single instant of time . . . there was nothing.

In darkness and without pain, Kerrigan collapsed partially on top of Feeny, the Minie ball that had shattered his skull lodged deep inside his brain.

He had not heard the blast of his own rifle or known whether he had even managed to fire it.

Nor did he feel himself die.

There had been no time to feel or know anything.

Joseph Kerrigan had merely stepped through a doorway into eternity.

"Joseph? Can you hear me?" Feeny said.

He knew there would be no answer.

More alone in the midst of a roaring battlefield than he had ever felt in his most solitary moments, Feeny was used up. Every man has a limit, and he'd reached his.

His panic became mindless and he pushed Kerrigan's mutilated corpse away from him.

Against all the dictates of logic and common sense, Feeny turned to run as if he could outpace the flying bullets chasing him.

He could not, of course.

Feeny felt something like a sledgehammer crash into the small of his back, and he pitched forward, momentum slamming his face hard into the bloodstained earth. He groaned, tried to stand, and felt a searing pain in his right leg. Looking down, he saw a nightmare of blood and shattered bone before he collapsed onto the ground.

Then all went quiet and still and he neither saw nor heard.

For Michael Feeny, late of County Mayo, Ireland, the Battle of Shiloh, just aborning into history, was over.

CHAPTER THREE

Kate Kerrigan rose from her chair and returned her husband's letter to her writing desk.

It had been brought, no, the word was smuggled, to her by Michael Feeny, who arrived in Nashville more dead than alive from a wound received at Shiloh.

She'd been poor then, and all the poorer for her husband's death, but Kate had a family to care for and playing the weeping widow and living off the charity of others had never entered her thinking.

Still, it had been a long, long time since she'd filled a bucket with water, soap, and a scrubbing brush.

The blood of the dead robber and would-be rapist still stained her bedroom rug and she could not abide the thought of it remaining there.

She was at the foot of the grand staircase, bucket in hand, when someone slammed the brass doorknocker hard . . . once, twice, three times.

Kate's revolver was in the parlor and she retrieved it, then returned to the door as a man's hand — for surely a woman would not have knocked so loudly? — hammered the knocker again.

"Who is it?" Kate said, her voice steady. The triple click of her Colt was loud in the quiet. "I warn you I put my faith in forty-fives."

A moment's pause, then, "Miz Kerrigan, it's me, Ma'am, Hiram Street, as ever was."

Kate recognized the voice of one of her top hands and unlocked the door.

"Come inside, Hiram," she said.

Street was a short, stocky man with sandy hair and bright hazel eyes.

He was a good, steady hand with a weakness for whiskey and whores, but Kate did not hold that against him.

"I was on my way back from town and met Sheriff Martin on the trail and he told me what happened," Street said. "I rode here as fast as I could to see if you needed help."

Kate pretended to be annoyed.

"Running my horses again, Hiram?"

"Well, I figgered this was an emergency, Miz Kerrigan, begging your pardon."

The cowboy wore a mackinaw and a wool muffler over his hat, tied in a huge knot under his chin.

He looked frozen stiff.

"Were you drinking at the Happy Reb again?" Kate said.

"I can tell you no lie, Ma'am. I sure was, but I only had but two dollars and that don't go far at Dan Pardee's prices."

"Come in and I'll get you a drink, Hiram. You look as cold as a bar owner's heart."

"Dan Pardee's anyway," Street said as he stepped inside.

He looked around at the marble, gold and red velvet of Ciarogan's vast receiving hall and said, "I ain't never been in the big house before, Ma'am. Takes a man's breath away."

Kate smiled.

"It wasn't always like this, Hiram, back in the day."

"You mean when you fit Comanches, Miz Kerrigan. I heard that."

Kate nodded.

"Comanches, Apaches, rustlers, claim jumpers, gunmen of all kinds and ambitions, even Mexican bandits raiding across the Rio Grande. Yes, I fought them all and killing one never troubled my sleep at night."

"Maybe that's why I'm a mite uneasy about that there iron you got in your hand, Ma'am," Street said.

"Oh, sorry, Hiram." Kate smiled and let the revolver hang by her side. "Please come into the parlor."

Street, with that solemn politeness punchers have around respectable women, and with many a *Beggin' your pardon, Ma'am* asked if he could remove his hat and coat.

"And should I take off my spurs, Miz Kerrigan?" he said. "I don't want to scratch your furniture, like."

"My sons don't take them off, so I don't see why you should," Kate said.

"Ciarogan is sure quiet tonight, Ma'am," Street said, accepting a chair and then a bourbon. "That's why that no-good saddle tramp came here."

"As you know, my sons are out on the range and Misses Ivy and Shannon are helping Lucy Cobb give birth. I also gave the servants the night off."

"Got fences down everywhere, but Mr. Trace told me to stay to home on account you'd be here alone," Street said. "I'm real sorry I left, Miz Kerrigan."

"How were you to know what would happen this evening, Hiram? Though I'll make no fuss about your lapse this time, don't do it again."

"Never, Ma'am, I swear it."

"Then we'll let the matter drop. I'll tell Trace that I sent you into town on an errand."

"I appreciate that, Ma'am. He has a temper, has Mr. Trace."

"Ah, he takes after me," Kate said.

Street hurriedly took a sip of his whiskey and said nothing.

Then, "Miz Kerrigan, I haven't been riding for Ciarogan long, but I'd like to hear about how it all started." Street smiled. "You got the only four pillar plantation house in Texas, I reckon."

"I doubt that," Kate said. "But I started with a small cabin and a thousand acres of scrub," Kate said.

Street spoke into the silence that followed.

"Ma'am, I'd like to hear the story of how you got here."

"Really, Hiram? Do you want to hear my story or do you like being close to the Old Crow bottle and warm fire?"

Street's smile was bright and genuine.

"Truth to tell, both," he said. "But I'm a man who loves a good story. I figger to get educated some day and become one of them dime novel authors."

"A very laudable ambition, Hiram," Kate said.

She thought for a few moments, then said, "Very well, I won't sleep tonight after what happened and the servants won't be back until late, so I'll tell you the story of Ciarogan and what went before."

Kate smiled. "But you have to sing for your supper, Hiram."

"Ma'am?"

"There's a bucket of water and scrubbing brush at the foot of the stairs and I have a rug in my bedroom that needs cleaning."

Street had the puncher's deep-seated dread of work he couldn't do off the back of a horse, but Miz Kerrigan was not a woman to be denied.

"Follow me," she said.

Street grabbed the soapy, slopping bucket and followed Kate up the staircase, his face grim, like a man climbing the steps to the gallows.

Wide-eyed, the cowboy stared at the bloodstained rug.

"Him?" he said.

"Him."

"Gut shot, Ma'am?"

"I didn't take time to see where my bullet hit."

"But look at the rug, Miz Kerrigan."

"I see it, Hiram. That's why you're here."

"But Ma'am, it looks like Miles Martin and his deputies tramped blood everywhere. The tracks of big policeman feet are all over the rug."

"Then you have your work cut out for you, Hiram. Have you not?"

Street made a long-suffering face, like a repentant sinner.

"This is because I rode off and left you alone, Miz Kerrigan. Ain't it?"

Kate smiled.

"Why Hiram, whatever gave you that idea?"

After an hour, many buckets of water, and a good deal of muttered cursing, Hiram Street threw the last bucketful of pink-tinted water outside and returned to the parlor.

"All done, Miz Kerrigan," he said.

Kate put aside the volume of Mr. Dickens she'd been reading and rose to her feet.

"I'll take a look," she said.

Kate cast a critical eye over the wet rug and said, "There, Hiram, in the corner. You missed a spot."

"Sorry Ma'am," Street said.

He got down on his knees and industrially scrubbed the offending stain with the heel of his hand. The spot was only the size of a dime, but Kate's eagle eyes missed nothing.

"Very well, Hiram," she said. "Now, we'll let the rug dry. I'll use one of the guestrooms for a few days."

Once the chastened cowboy was again sitting by the fire, a glass of whiskey in hand, Kate smiled at him.

"Do you still wish to hear the story of Kate Kerrigan, her life and times?"

Street settled his shoulders into the leather and nodded.

"I sure do, Ma'am."

"I'll tell you of my early days, when just staying alive was a struggle. To relate all that's passed in the last forty years would be too long in the telling."

Kate flashed her dazzling smile and continued to do so.

"I'm sure there's enough material in the story of my younger days for a hundred dime novels," she said.

"Beggin' your pardon, Ma'am, but I'm eager to hear the tale of Kate Kerrigan," Street said.

"Then, Hiram, you shall at least hear some of it."

CHAPTER FOUR

A heavy pounding at the door woke Kate Kerrigan from sleep.

Beside her on the bed, Shannon, her youngest child, stirred and Kate whispered, "Shush, my little darling, go back to sleep."

The girl smiled, revealing dimples on her cheeks — where the angels had kissed her as a baby, Kate had told her — and was instantly asleep again.

The door rattled in its frame under further pounding and Kate rose and threw a threadbare pink robe over her equally worn nightgown.

So as not to disturb the children, she opened the door and, barefoot, stepped into the cold of the Nashville morning.

Big Fin Gannon, his huge, red, whiskey face bookended by frizzy, muttonchop side-whiskers, stood on the sidewalk, the enamel jug Kate had left outside her door in his hand.

"This will be the last milk you'll get from me, Kate Kerrigan, until you pay my score," Gannon said.

"You and the butcher, the baker, and the candle-stick maker will all get paid when I have the money, Fin Gannon, and you know it. Kate Kerrigan always pays her due."

Behind the dairyman, blurred by mist, the huge blond Percheron in the traces of the milk cart snorted, as though he put little faith in Kate's promises.

"Look at you Kate, as beautiful a woman as ever walked the streets of this city, yet you're content to live in a hovel and let your children go hungry," Gannon said.

"I go hungry, that is true, but my children . . . never," Kate said.

Gannon sighed and rolled his eyes.

"Kate Kerrigan, how many times have I offered to take you to wife?"

"Every time you deliver the milk."

"I'm not a rich man, but I can offer you a brick house and a maid to take care of your needs."

"And my children?"

"Yes, and them, too, if you'll only consent to my proposal of marriage."

"I'll add you to my list of suitors, Fin Gannon."

"Then put me to the top of the list, Kate,

where I belong."

Gannon handed over the jug, then reached into his pocket and brought out a paper bag.

"Here, take your milk, and some molasses candy for the little ones. And don't forget my score now."

The big man turned and stepped toward his wagon.

"Fin," Kate said.

Gannon stopped, his face expectant.

"Thank you," Kate said. "And if you ever pound like an avenging angel on my door again, I'll take a stick to you."

The big man laughed.

"God strike me, but you're a woman any man could be proud of, Kate Kerrigan. Unless I miss my guess, you'll tread a wide path some day."

Kate Kerrigan added fresh coffee, and not much of that, to the three-day-old grounds already in the pot. She added water she'd pumped from the communal well the day before and set the pot on the stove to boil.

The girls were still asleep, as was Ivy's twin brother Niall, but Trace and Quinn had left earlier to go to work.

Her sons prided themselves that when they rose and dressed, they never wakened their mother or the young 'uns.

But Kate always woke, and worried, though she never told that to her sons.

She stepped to the single window that overlooked Barnes Street, a narrow lane in the impoverished warren of tenements that made up Nashville's Sixth Ward Black Bottom slum district.

As the poor struggled to survive, Black Bottom filled up with saloons, whorehouses, and gambling joints, adding to the violent crime and nightly murders that made the area a living hell.

Despite stinking outdoor toilets and coal stoves and fireplaces that covered everything in soot, Kate Kerrigan rose above the squalor and, with the optimism of the Irish, kept her eyes fixed on ONE DAY . . . the day she and the children would leave this poverty behind and move on to a better life.

Kate stared out at the mist that moved through the street like a gray ghost.

The studded working boots of a passerby clattered on the cobbles, but the man himself was lost in the fog.

As she often did, Kate Kerrigan wondered if God had taken a dislike to her and that the Blessed Virgin had turned her back on she and her family.

But a frown gathered between her beautiful eyes as she told herself she was blasphemous for allowing such thoughts to enter her head.

God was God, after all, surely under no obligation to answer to a simple young Irishwoman who, when she thought about it, had to admit she had received some fine blessings along with lots of intolerable difficulties.

Now one of those blessings, Shannon, sat up in bed and knuckled her eyes.

"Has the bad man gone, Mama?" she said.

Kate smiled and sat on the bed beside the child.

"He's gone. It was only Fin Gannon bringing the milk." She tickled Shannon and made her giggle. "And he brought candy for you and Ivy."

"Can I have it?" the child said, her little face eager.

"After breakfast. Rye bread and fresh milk to dip it in. Now isn't that your very best favorite?"

Shannon nodded.

"Good. Then that's settled. Breakfast first and candy afterward."

The little girl scrambled out of bed, smiling, the child's innocent embrace of a new aborning day and of the great adventures to come.

Kate glanced at the bed and the pillows

where her husband had once laid his head and thought it looked like such a lonely place.

He would never sleep there again.

Kate had lost him five years before, the same year that Shannon had been born.

Joseph Kerrigan now lay in a grave known only to God and Kate's youngest daughter was the last part of himself he'd left her before he went off to die.

It struck Kate how tragic it was that little Shannon was so associated with death, even in her very name.

She'd been named after Kate's younger sister, Shannon Marie Cotter, whose tragic fate had caused Kate's heartbroken father to move his family from the slums of New York to the slums of Nashville.

Shannon's death had happened years ago, before the war and the death of her own husband, but the memory of it still tore at Kate's heart . . .

CHAPTER FIVE

Like many working Irish of the day, the Cotter family had lived in a crowded, stinking tenement in Five Points, an urban crossroad slum rife with squalor, stench, poverty, and crime.

The great novelist Charles Dickens visited the terrible place in 1842, and wrote:

What place is this to which the squalid street conducts us? A kind of square of leprous houses, some of which are attainable only by crazy wooden stairs without. What lies behind this tottering flight of steps? Let us go on again, and plunge into the Five Points.

This is the place; these narrow ways diverging to the right and left, and reeking everywhere with dirt and filth. Such lives as are led here, bear the same fruit as elsewhere. The coarse and bloated faces at the doors have counterparts at home

45

and all the world over.

Debauchery has made the very houses prematurely old. See how the rotten beams are tumbling down, and how the patched and broken windows seem to scowl dimly, like eyes that have been hurt in drunken forays. Many of these pigs live here. Do they ever wonder why their masters walk upright instead of going on all fours, and why they talk instead of grunting?

Dickens' visit made it the fashionable for upper crust New Yorkers, or tourists who wanted to emulate them, to take guided and protected tours of the world's most infamous slum, its only competition for filth, poverty, and wretchedness London's East End.

And it was here the Irish predominated, along with Germans, free blacks, Jews, Italians, and various other groups and nationalities.

Well-dressed and often accompanied by off-duty policemen or hired thugs, the lofty dandies and their satin and lace belles pranced along the dung-crusted and often bloodstained streets of the Points like visitors to a human zoo.

The rich ogled the poor, the wretched

unwashed around them, as though they believed that such human animals were incapable of realizing that they were both loathed and feared.

It was then that Kate, just sixteen and already a stunning beauty, was introduced to the true meaning of poverty. The deep wound it caused would stay with her the rest of her long life.

When parties of society "slummers" came through, the Cotters, a proud family descended from both Viking lords and Irish kings, generally found a way to vanish.

They'd usually duck behind a building, a cluster of people, or a parked wagon where they could avoid the shame of seeing the contempt in the eyes of their betters.

One fine spring day that Kate would always remember, she wore a patched but pretty gingham dress and a white straw hat with little pink flowers that her mother had bought her from a used clothing stall.

Kate Cotter looked at her smiling reflection in a store window and thought she looked like the Queen of the May.

But her happiness was not to last.

A pack of aristocratic slummers, children in tow, strolled past her with perfumed kerchiefs to their faces and their heads tilted back, so they literally were looking down their noses at the miserable ones around them.

A girl about the same age as Kate broke away from her parents and stared her with round, insolent brown eyes.

"Why are you such a raggedy doll?" the girl said. "Does your papa not have enough money to buy you pretty clothes?"

"I'm wearing pretty clothes," Kate said.

"No, you're not. You're raggedy and you don't smell nice."

Kate had first thought the girl, who was rather plain, her blond hair in pigtails, was merely curious. But now it seemed she was determined to be mean.

"My mama says you ragged, smelly people are not people at all, but some kind of wild animals," the girl said. "Is that true?"

Kate moved to walk on.

But, much to the amusement of the girl's wealthy parents, their daughter blocked her path and glanced to her fond mama and papa for approval.

Their silence and smiles granted it.

"Where do you live, dirty Raggedy?" the girl said. Her smile was nasty. "In a coal cellar?"

Kate's temper was always an uncertain thing and her pride had been cut to the quick.

She slammed her strong right hand into her tormentor's face and pushed . . . hard.

The girl shrieked and fell on her back, conveniently, Kate would later recall with glee, on a pile of steaming dung recently deposited by a passing draft horse.

The result was quick and inevitable.

One of the slummers' guardian thugs grabbed Kate by the back of her coat collar as the girl screamed and a gawping crowd gathered.

Within a couple of minutes, a very large and red-faced policeman appeared and the dung-covered girl's outraged mother shrieked at him, "She tried to kill my Alice! Hang her! Hang her straight away!"

Her anger flaring red-hot, Kate struggled with the thug and kicked at his shins.

She got a slap across the face for her pains that momentarily stunned her. The thug, a vicious brute with a knife-scarred face, drew back his fist for a crushing backhand but the copper's voice stopped him.

"Strike that child again, James McCoy, and you'll see the inside of a cell this day."

"She's a murderess!" Alice's mother yelled, holding her reeking, bawling daughter at arm's length.

"I'll be the judge of who's a murderer and who is not," the cop said.

The jostling crowd had little love for the police, but they'd far less for slummers, and now there were ominous mutters among them as they saw one of their own abused by their common enemies.

The cop's name was Sam Sullivan, a drinker and sometime bare-knuckle prize-fighter, and he was as Irish as the pigs o' Docherty.

He'd walked a Five Points beat these twenty years and had learned to tune into the mad, menacing music of an angry crowd.

He took Kate by the arm and said to Mc-Coy, "For God's sake get your charges out of here or they'll be torn to pieces."

McCoy could read the mood of a mob as well as Sullivan.

Working for despised outsiders, he'd struck a slum girl — and men had been strung up from lampposts for less.

The thug urged the slummers to leave, quietly and with no more fuss.

But the mother wasn't finished with the big, broken-nosed policeman just yet.

"Constable, my husband is a friend of the police commissioner, and if that murderous girl isn't hanged at short notice I'll see you lose your job and your pension," she said.

"You go to hell, you stuck-up sow!" Kate

yelled at the woman.

But Sullivan only bowed and smiled.

"Indeed, Ma'am? And where would his honor the commissioner find another Irishman crazy enough to walk this beat?"

That last remark tickled the crowd, and they cheered and laughed, then directed jeers in the direction of the Alice and her parents.

Angry Mother opened her mouth to speak again, but a handful of thrown horse dung splattered across her face and shut her up quick.

McCoy, his face ashen, grabbed the woman by the arm and yelled, "Run!"

The woman saw the writing on the wall as backs bent to pick up more manure . . . and rocks.

Alarmed and thoroughly scared, she and her husband grabbed their daughter and fled, the mother's white petticoats fluttering as she hiked up her skirts and her high-heeled boots kettle-drummed over the cobbles.

Only the good humor of the crowd and Sam Sullivan's significant, six-foot-four presence saved the slummers from further harm, though some young ragamuffins, hooting and hollering, gave chase for a block or two.

■ ■ ■ ■

"Now, young lady, you'll come along with me," Sullivan said.

"And you'll hang me, is that it?" Kate said. "Then my blood will be on your hands, Sam Sullivan."

"If you were a lad, I'd tell you hanging was too good for you, so I'd kick your arse," the cop said.

"You'd kick a girl, would you?" Kate said. "Just like a Sullivan, sheep-stealers and wife-beaters the lot of you. Just let go of my arm and I'll give you a fistfight to remember."

"I'll do no such thing, Kate Cotter," the big cop said. "I'll let your father deal with you. Such an honorable, law-abiding gentleman to have such a hellion of a daughter."

"No, throw me in a cold damp cell with the rats and the murderers," Kate said.

"Ah, then you're afraid you're father will take a stick to you," Sullivan said as he forced his way through the teeming streets, using Kate as a battering ram.

Bouncing off shoulders, poked by tattered parasols, Kate was incensed, boiling mad.

"I swear, Sam Sullivan, you've not heard the end of this," she said. "The next time I see you I'll beat you within an inch of your life for treating me so!"

The cop laughed, then said, "And here we are at your door, girl, and it's glad I'll be when I see the last of you."

Patrick Cotter was a mild-mannered man with the long, sensitive face of a martyred saint on the wall of a Gothic cathedral. He had failed at everything he'd tried, but was a poet by inclination, though none of his verses had ever found their way to print.

Now, after he'd listened to Sam Sullivan's story and had bid the big constable a cordial good day, he stared at his daughter and read the defiance in her eyes.

"She called me dirty and raggedy," Kate said. "I should have socked her, not pushed her."

"Dirty you're not, raggedy, well, we could argue that point," Cotter said. "But it's a fine thing for the police to come to my very door with my oldest daughter's arms clamped to her side like a common criminal."

"Sam Sullivan refused to fight me, Pa," Kate said. "I would have shown him a thing or two."

"Young ladies don't fistfight with policemen," her father said. "They get married,

53

have children, and become dutiful wives and mothers. That is the natural order of things, Kate."

Cotter glanced out the window into the squalid street.

"Though, I'll admit, there's little natural order in Five Points."

"Then why do we stay in this place?" Kate said.

"Because for now it's our home. We'll leave one day, Kate, when I'm offered a better situation than warehouse clerk. I swear it on your sainted mother."

"It can't come soon enough for me, Pa," Kate said. "I want to look out my bedroom window and see trees."

"And so do I, my dear, so do I."

Pat Cotter's face took on a serious expression.

"You won't go out again unless I am with you, Kate. Do you understand?"

Kate nodded and touched her father's, slender, ink-stained hand.

"Pa, I wouldn't hurt you or bring disgrace to you for all the world."

"Nor I you," her father said.

That day neither father nor daughter could foresee the dark cloud that gathered on their horizon, and the horrific events that

would end Kate's childhood in a tempest of
rape, vengeance, and death.

Chapter Six

Shannon Cotter, Kate's fourteen-year-old sister, was a willful, intelligent girl with a love of the fiddle music she often heard spilling from the saloons and the works of Sir Walter Scott, represented by a couple of volumes her father had not as yet consigned to a pawnbroker.

Not as beautiful as Kate, she was pretty nonetheless with the bright blue eyes and blond hair of a Nordic ancestor.

But what drew the ogling attention of young men was her fully developed body, especially her bust that was large and high, and the lovely straight line of her slender back.

Shannon, eager to escape the gloomy confines of the tenements, often strolled the streets alone, trusting to daylight and the constant crowds jostling for space on the sidewalks.

On one such day, a brewers' dray, drawn

by two shire horses, accidentally mounted the sidewalk in front of her and Shannon stepped into an open doorway to avoid getting crushed.

"Watch where you're going!" the driver yelled at her. "Damned daydreamer!"

Shannon was about to yell back that it was his fault, not hers, when a large, hairy forearm clamped around her throat.

The man dragged her backward into a dark stairwell and said, "Shut your trap, girlie, and do as your told or I'll rip your heart out."

It was an Irish accent, but born of Five Points, not the home country.

"She's prime, Bill," another man said.

"A beauty, lay to that," said a second, talking through a grin.

Both were Americans, and sounded like seamen.

"Get her upstairs, Bill," the first speaker said. "And ye can have the first go."

The man called Bill dragged Shannon up stone steps that led to the upper floors of what was an abandoned warehouse.

The stairwell smelled of piss and stale vomit and was so dark the girl couldn't see her abductors.

But she knew what was in store for her and she screamed.

Who in Five Points ever paid heed to a woman's screams, a sound as familiar as the wails of hungry children or the chirp of a house sparrow?

The men hauled the terrified girl into a top floor room. Its windows were boarded and the room was as black as ink.

One man lit a match and touched fire to a candle stub stuck onto a chipped blue plate that lay on the floor.

A couple of rats scuttled from the light as Shannon was thrown onto a pile of rags in the corner.

She lay on her back, stunned for a moment, and then got up on one elbow.

"Let me go and I'll give you a dollar," she said, her lower lip trembling.

"You don't have a dollar," the man called Bill said, slipping his suspender off his shoulders.

"I do so," Shannon said, frantic now. "My father has a dollar and he'll give it to you."

The man pulled down his filthy long johns, exposing himself.

"After you've had a taste of this, you won't talk of dollars," he said.

By the feeble, guttering glow of the candle, Shannon Cotter was raped.

The rats gathered in the corners and looked on, their whiskered noses twitching, and men breathed heavily, saliva glistening on their chins, and waited their turn.

A quick rainstorm showered, passed on, and the eaves ticked water. A train bell clanged in the distance and then a man gasped, spent.

Shannon knew this ordeal would inevitably end in her death.

And as a second man threw himself on top of her, she wished fervently to die very soon, without more pain . . . just close her eyes . . . and . . . let . . . herself . . . go . . .

The man rolled off of her.

"Now she's all yours, Tom," he said, getting to his feet. He looked down at Shannon and said, "Enjoying it now, ain't you, girlie? Well, there's more to come, lay to that."

The man called Tom, drunker than the others, swigged down what was left of his whiskey and tossed the empty bottle into a corner where it smashed and startled the rats.

He fumbled with his buttons, tried to pull down his pants and fell over onto his side. A heavy man, the floor shook, and his companions laughed.

"You're too drunk, Tom," Bill said. "You've lost your turn."

The man got to his knees and then struggled to his feet.

"Damn you, I'll do her," he said. He pulled a Bowie from the sheath on his belt. "And by God, I'll gut any man who stands in my way."

"Step aside, Tom," Bill said. "If there's any gutting to be done, I'll be the one that does it."

Tom grinned, his face a devilish mask.

"You're a rum one, Bill, rum as ever was," he said. "But don't stand in my way or I'll cut your whore, then no one will have her."

Bill pulled a knife, as did the third man.

"Two against one, is it?" Tom said. "Then let's be having you."

Tom lunged at Bill, who parried and cut back, drawing blood.

The fight then became general and the three men stabbed and slashed at one another, fighting for the sheer love of it.

Shannon saw her chance.

She grabbed the dress they had torn from her and made it out the door. She was halfway down the stairs before she tripped and tumbled to the next landing.

Knowing what horrors lay behind her, the girl scrambled to her feet and made it to the doorway.

Shannon hurriedly buttoned herself into what remained of her dress, and ran into the street.

Her cries for help went unheeded.

What the passersby saw was just another whore beaten by her pimp.

It was no concern of theirs, or the law.

CHAPTER SEVEN

When Shannon got home she managed to contrive a story to explain the ruination of her dress and the bruising and abrasion of her body.

"A man tried to rob me," she said. "I fought him off, but he tore my dress and threw me to the ground."

Patrick Cotter accepted the explanation, an everyday occurrence in Five Points, but Kate looked into her sister's wounded eyes and saw something much more serious.

She later took Shannon aside and said, "Now tell me the truth about happened."

"I told you the truth," the girl said.

"Shannon, did a boy try to abuse you?" Kate said.

Shannon heaved a great shuddering sigh.

"Not a boy," she said.

Her stomach tying itself in knots, Kate waited.

It took a while before Shannon spoke again.

"Three men," she said.

She threw herself into Kate's arms.

"Two of them . . . they dragged me into a room and . . . and . . ."

Kate said nothing.

She hugged her sister close, her beautiful face like stone.

"Name them," she said.

Shannon drew back and looked at her sister in surprise.

She'd never before heard ice in Kate's voice or seen the black flame in her eyes.

"I don't know," Shannon said.

"Give me names," Kate said.

"One was called Bill, I think he was Irish. Another was Tom and I didn't hear the third man's name."

"Tell nothing of this to Father." Kate said. "He's a good man, but he's not cut out for this kind of work."

"Kate, what kind of work?" Shannon said.

"The work that now falls on me," Kate said.

Two days later, walking through rain, Kate sought out Sam Sullivan.

The big cop wore a rain cape and stood in the doorway of Nathan Goldberg's used clothing store on Swan Street.

"Have you come to fight me, then, Kate Cotter?" he said, smiling.

The girl did not smile back, but she stepped beside him.

"I need your help, Constable Sullivan," Kate said.

"Now it's Constable Sullivan is it? You must need my help real bad."

"I need to find three men who run together, probably were sailors at one time."

"Now why would you be seeking out men like that, Kate?"

The girl ignored his comment.

"One is called Bill, an Irishman, another is Tom. I don't know the third one's name," she said.

"Why are you asking me this?" Sullivan said.

"Why is she asking you this?" said Nathan Goldberg who was standing at Kate's shoulder.

"This is no business of yours, Nathan," Sullivan said.

"It is my business if a huge policeman is standing on my doorstep, blocking the way of my customers."

"It's raining, Mr. Goldberg. You don't have any customers," Kate said.

"And what if the reason is that a huge

policeman is standing in my doorway?"

"Then I'll move on," Sullivan said.

"Yes, take yourself off," Goldberg said. "But come back for coffee at three, Sam."

"Who's in charge of the coffee today, Nathan? You or your wife?"

"Rachel is here today, minding a store with no customers."

"Then I'll come back," Sullivan said.

As he and Kate walked away, Goldberg called, "We'll have rugelach. So bring your young lady, Sam."

The rain grew harder and the ominous black and gray clouds that filled the sky over Five Points promised a lot more to come. In the distance thunder rumbled.

"You never answered me, Kate," Sullivan said. "Why are you asking me about mariners?"

"I can't tell you, but it's a serious matter and of the greatest moment."

"You're soaked to the skin," Sullivan said.

"That's how important it is that I find these three men," Kate said.

"Under the awning here," the big cop said.

For a few moments he stared at the rain making startled Vs all over the cobbled street, his face frowning in concentration.

Then he said, "The only three men I can think of are Bill Wooten, Tom Van Meter, and Chauncey Upsell. They were sailors on the same ship and now they run together, whore together and, if the truth be known, roll drunks together."

Sullivan turned his attention to Kate and said, "Come to think of it, I saw Chauncey and Bill yesterday and they were cut up some."

Shannon had told Kate about the knife fight and she knew she had found her men.

"Where do they drink?" she said.

"Always at the Cross Keys on Kelley Street. They can go in the book there."

Sullivan shoved an arm out from under the awning and let the rain fall on his hand.

Without turning, he said, "What happened, Kate?"

The girl knew that now was the time for the truth.

"Two of them, I believe Wooten and Upsell, raped my sister. Van Meter was too drunk to try."

"Young Shannon says this terrible thing?"

"Yes, she does."

"Saying and proving are two different things, especially in Five Points."

"I know that."

"Kate Cotter, I'll try to find out what I can. That's why you're here, isn't it, to ask my help?"

"Yes," Kate said. "Yes, it is."

"Then I'll see if I can get a detective interested in the case," the cop said. "But I warn you now, a rape in this area usually goes without investigation."

Kate hesitated, fearing that Sullivan might suspect something, but she had another question to ask.

"Is Ben Hollister still in town?"

"Goodness, girl, what do you want with such a man?" Sullivan said.

"He was a friend of my father's," Kate said, which was true.

Hollister was a gambler who'd worked the Mississippi steamboats, then fell on hard times. He used to visit Kate's father regularly since they both had an interest in literature, but she hadn't seen him in several months.

It was said that Hollister was a notorious dueler back in the old days and had killed eight men, but her pa said that number was probably exaggerated.

"Yes, he's still in Five Points," Sullivan said. "He firmly believes he can outrun a losing streak that started years ago, but of course he can't. The toughs and gangs around here leave him alone, though. He has a reputation as a bad man to tangle with."

The cop stared hard at Kate.

"And a bad man for you to tangle with," he said.

"My pa wants me to return one of Mr. Hollister's books," Kate said. "That's all."

"He still lives on Birmingham Lane, but bring the book to me and I'll give it to him," Sullivan said. "The lane isn't a safe place for a young lady."

"Yes, I'll do that," Kate said. "And you'll let me know . . ."

"If anything comes up? Yes, I will."

The girl whispered her thanks and stepped into the rain.

"Kate!" Sullivan called after her.

She turned and waited.

"I'm sorry, Kate, so damned sorry."

Kate Cotter nodded.

"And so am I, Constable Sullivan."

CHAPTER EIGHT

Birmingham Lane was a narrow alley between four-story tenements, the upper apartments accessed by outside, rickety wooden stairs. It was a foul, impoverished place where pigs still roamed and its people lived lives of quiet desperation.

As Kate Kerrigan remembered, Ben Hollister lived on the ground floor and his door was splintered by three bullet holes, now healing over thanks to time and weather.

Kate recalled her father telling her that Hollister had killed a man attempting to steal his brass doorknocker. The three holes made a clover shape that could be covered by a silver dollar and bore eloquent testimony to the gambler's aim and temperament.

Her heart thudding in her chest, Kate used the polished knocker and a moment later a man's voice reached her from inside.

"Go away."

"I'll do no such thing," Kate said. "This is Kate Cotter and I demand to speak with you."

"Patrick's daughter?"

"As ever was."

"Hold on a minute."

Locks clicked and chains rattled, then the door opened and a tall, slender man, somewhere in the far side of his forties, stood smiling at her.

"I declare, it's young Miss Cotter," he said. "I haven't seen you, in what? A year, at least. You've grown prettier."

Kate gave a little curtsey.

"Thank you, sir. I'm desirous of talking with you."

"Then enter, and welcome," Hollister said.

With considerable Southern charm, he bowed Kate into a small parlor, sparsely furnished but swept and clean. A hand-tinted lithograph of a Mississippi steamboat hung over the fireplace.

"I apologize that my present circumstances do not allow me to properly welcome such an honored guest," Hollister said. "But I can offer you a glass of port, if that is to your taste."

"A glass of port would be most welcome," Kate said.

"Then first let me divest you of your coat,

Miss Cotter. It seems you've walked far in the rain."

"Indeed I have, sir," Kate said.

After the girl was seated with her drink, Hollister smiled at her, waiting for her to speak.

He was a very handsome man with a refined Anglo Saxon face, a carefully barbered shock of brown hair and a fine mustache. His clothes were much patched but had once been expensive and spoke of people and places beyond Kate's imagining.

Finally Hollister broke the silence.

"How is your father? It's been a while since my last visit."

"He is well, sir."

"And your sister?"

Kate fumbled for words, hesitated, and stayed silent.

Although he detected something amiss, Hollister's breeding as a Southern gentleman would not allow him to press the matter.

"Then, what can I do for you, Miss Cotter? Consider me your obedient servant."

Kate took a bolstering sip of port.

"I need to borrow a pistol, Mr. Hollister," she said. "I know you have such a thing."

The gambler was surprised and it showed in his shocked blue eyes.

"Good lord, young lady, whatever for? What a most singular request."

Kate recalled a phrase she'd read in a newspaper, one that Hollister would understand.

"It's an affair of honor, sir," she said.

Hollister was silent for few moments, then spoke.

"I suspect that this is an *affaire du coeur* that involves your lovely sister Shannon," he said. "But I will not pursue the matter."

"May I have the pistol?" Kate said, her chin determined.

The gambler sighed, like a man recalling a bad memory.

"Miss Cotter, have you ever killed a man?"

Kate shook her head,

"No, I have not."

"There's no going back from a killing," Hollister said. "After the deed is done, not all your tears, not all your prayers, can bring a man back again."

Kate said nothing.

"For the rest of your life you live with it," Hollister said.

"I protect mine," Kate said. "And when I fail to protect them, I will exact vengeance for them."

"Your father knows of this?"

"No, he does not."

"Patrick is not a violent man."

"He is a poet," Kate said. "Poets do not make good . . . avengers."

Hollister rose and stepped to a dresser. He opened the bottom drawer and brought out a rectangular walnut case.

He opened the case and revealed the contents to Kate.

A beautiful blue revolver with an elegant side mounted hammer nestled in red velvet along with a powder flask, percussion caps, round balls, and paper cartridges.

"This is a Model 1855 revolver designed by a Colt gunsmith named Elijah Root. It shoots a .31 caliber ball and I had the barrel cut back to three inches."

"Will it suit my purpose?" Kate said.

"I don't know what your purpose is," Hollister said.

"I think you do, sir," Kate said.

"God help me, I guess I have an idea," Hollister said. "I have other revolvers, but they are far larger. The Root can be easily concealed."

The gambler closed the case lid.

"I'll load it for you before you leave. Make sure the powder stays dry."

"I appreciate this, Mr. Hollister," Kate said.

He shook his head.

"My God, you're only a slip of a girl."

"As I told you before, I fight for what's mine," Kate said.

"The Root is not a man killer. You'll need to be close and aim for the broadest part of a man's body. Don't try a headshot, it's too difficult and you only have five shots."

"How close?" Kate said.

"Within spitting distance," Hollister said.

He stared at the girl.

"Changed your mind?"

Kate shook her head.

Hollister smiled. "You've got bark on you, Miss Cotter."

"Someone in my family needs it," Kate said.

"Your father has sand, but in a different, quieter way. He's not what the Mexicans call a *pistolero.*"

"Am I, do you think?"

"You have the makings, Miss Cotter. I sense a courage and a ruthlessness in you that I've sensed in few men."

CHAPTER NINE

The evening after Kate Cotter's meeting
with Ben Hollister her father retired to bed
early with a bad cold.

Kate quickly changed into a modest green
cotton dress with a high collar and threw
her late mother's cloak over her shoulders.

The dress had two deep pockets in front
and into one of those she slipped the Colt
that she'd hidden in her underwear drawer.
The white straw hat completed her outfit,
and she decided she looked like an innocent
country girl just arrived in Five Points.

Shannon, still recovering from her ordeal,
was asleep, whimpering every now and then
as her bad dreams returned and tormented
her.

Kate kissed her sister on the cheek and
then slipped out of the house.

According to the clock on the mantel it
was ten o'clock.

The moon rode high in a star-strewn sky

and made the slate roofs of the tenements glow like tarnished silver.

Her button boots loud on the cobbles, Kate walked in the direction of Kelley Street, through throngs of people, men, women, and children and lovers walking arm in arm.

The residents of Five Points were in no hurry to return to their hot, smelly, rat-infested apartments and preferred to remain outside at night for as long as they could.

A few men hurled suggestive, grinning comments at Kate as she passed, but she walked on, looking straight ahead.

Kelley Street was no better and no worse than any other thoroughfare in the area, but there were fewer tenements and more grim, sooty warehouses, some of them abandoned and boarded, echoing with street noises.

Kate looked around her. It was in one of those buildings . . .

She put the thought out of her head.

It was time to act the foolish virgin.

The Cross Keys saloon was a smoky, noisy gin mill that smelled of sweaty, unwashed bodies, cheap perfume, spilled beer, and the usual background fragrance of urine and vomit.

Kate had her bottom pinched five times

before she reached the long, mahogany bar, backed by six bartenders with slicked down hair and diamond stickpins in their cravats.

When one of the bartenders, among the aristocracy of Five Points, deigned to look in Kate's direction, she dropped a little curtsey and ordered a small sherry, "Sir, if you please."

"I'll pay that for the little lady," said a rough-edged voice said behind her.

A huge, hairy forearm reached out and grabbed the sherry glass. It looked like a tiny, amber wild-flower in his hand.

Kate turned and looked into the middle button of a man's plaid shirt.

She raised her eyes and saw a broad, red-veined face and fleshy wide nose broken to a pulp. The man had heavy-lidded eyes, pendulous, unshaven jowls and the chest and shoulders of a village blacksmith.

He seemed as huge and indestructible as a German ironclad.

Kate thought of the revolver in her pocket and feared that its tiny ball would bounce off such a man and do him no more harm than a stinging gnat.

"So what brings you to Five Points, dearie?" the man said, his hand already tracing the curve of Kate's hip.

She played her role to the hilt.

"Oh kind sir, I've just arrived from old Ireland and I'm looking for a place to lay my poor head," she said.

"Well, am I not from the old country my ownself?" the man said. "And is my name not Bill Wooten? We are well met, indeed."

It was only now Kate noticed that he had a fresh cut across his low, brutish forehead. He was one of them. One of the rapists.

She had thought it might take days to find him, but here he was, big and bold as brass.

"I have the very place for you," the man said. "It's a boardinghouse run by as respectable a lady as you'll ever find." He winked. "No gentleman callers, if such are to your liking."

"Oh no, sir," Kate said. "It has been in my mind of late to enter holy orders."

"Is that so?" Wooten said. "And you'll make a fine nun, I'll be bound."

He grabbed Kate's arm in his huge meaty fist.

"Come and meet my friends, two Catholic, churchgoing gentlemen as ever was, lay to that."

As Wooten half-dragged Kate to a table, he shouldered a slatternly woman aside. She smiled at the girl, revealing black teeth and said, "Watch your step, dearie."

"Away with you," Wooten growled, drawing back his hand.

The woman scampered away and the man said, "Me and my friends have been trying to save that fallen woman's soul, but she'll have none of it."

The two men who sat at the table, their sullen faces much cut about by knives, stared at Kate as Wooten shoved her in a chair.

"My associates," the big man said. "The one with the white eye is Tom Van Meter and t'other with the warts all over his ugly mug is Chauncey Upsell."

Van Meter smiled at Kate.

"We may look rough and ready, but we're honest men to the bone," he said. "Ain't that right, Chauncey?"

"To the bone all right," Upsell said, grinning.

His eyes had already stripped Kate naked.

"And what's your name, dearie?" Van Meter said.

"Why sir, it's Mary. Mary Brennan," Kate said.

"Little Mary has just arrived from the Emerald Isle and she's looking for a place to stay," Wooten said. "I thought we might take her along to Mrs. O'Hara's boardin'house."

He smiled at Kate.

"You're not safe in the streets by yourself."

Upsell, his eyes fixed on Kate's breasts, touched his tongue to his top lip.

"I say we leave now," he said. "Mrs. O'Hara locks her door early."

"Good idea," Van Meter said.

He grinned at Kate.

"You'll be safe with us, Mary me darlin'."

Kate Cotter knew she was headed into the lion's den.

The Colt, heavy in her pocket, gave her little reassurance.

She'd never shot a gun before, never killed a man.

It came to her then that it might be the last night of her life.

But as the three vile thugs pushed Kate along the street she knew that, given the choice, she'd do it all over again.

The animals had harmed her own and there was no stepping away from that.

Not now.

Not ever.

The events that followed after Kate left the pub played out exactly as she feared and knew they would.

Oddly silent, but constantly exchanging grins, as the three men walked her closer to what seemed an abandoned warehouse they began to glance over their shoulders.

Satisfied that there were no prying eyes on the street, they stopped, and with considerable violence dragged Kate into a doorway.

Van Meter kicked the door open and threw her into a dark, echoing stairwell.

"Oh sirs, what are you doing?" Kate cried out. "This is not Mrs. O'Hara's."

"You can go there later," Bill Wooten said.

"If ye can walk, that is," Upsell said.

"Please," Kate said, "I am a virgin, destined for the nunnery."

"Not for much longer," Van Meter said.

"Me first," Upsell said. "Girlie, I'm gonna bust you wide open."

Convinced they had a terrified, cowering victim in their power, the grinning Wooten thumbed a match into flame and lit a stub of candle he'd picked up from the bottom step.

For a moment, no one had a hand on Kate.

"Damn you all to hell!" she yelled.

The gun was in her hands and she fired.

The bullet hit Wooten high in the chest and he fell back, gawping at the blood pumping out of him.

Deafened, her ears ringing, Kate thumbed

back the hammer again, wondering at how steady was her hand.

Van Meter charged toward her, cursing, his clawed hands reaching for Kate's throat.

Ben Hollister had warned Kate never to try for a head shot.

The light was poor, but the candle Wooten had dropped was still alight and had tinted the blackness with a pale yellow haze.

Kate's ball, fired at a distance of a couple of feet, crashed in the thug's forehead and dropped him like a felled steer.

Chauncey Upsell yelled that he was out of it.

Like the other two who sprawled on the floor, one dead, the second coughing up frothing blood, Upsell was a skull and knuckle fighter and good with the blade against any opponent.

But fighting with a gun was alien to him.

Her revolver had turned a hundred pound girl into more than his equal and even now, as he saw death in her eyes, he couldn't grasp what was happening to him.

"Her name was Shannon. I am her sister," Kate said. "You raped her."

"No . . ." Upsell said. "I didn't . . . I couldn't . . ."

"You watched these two animals rape her and did nothing."

82

"I'm sorry. Put the gun away and I'll buy your drink."

"It's way too late for sorrow, Upsell. Yours and mine."

She shot into the man's belly, fired again and watched him fall.

Gunsmoke fogged the stairwell as Kate stepped to Wooten.

The man was still alive.

"For God's sake get me a doctor," he said, his eyes wild. "I don't want to die."

Kate spat on him.

She had one ball left. . . .

The one Bill Wooten rode into hell.

CHAPTER TEN

A few days later Constable Sam Sullivan met Kate Cotter in the street.

"Did you hear?" he said.

"Hear what?" Kate said, her eyelashes fluttering her innocence.

"Bill Wooten, Tom Van Meter, and Chauncey Upsell are all dead," the big cop said. "Shot down in an abandoned warehouse on Kelley Street."

"Then good riddance," Kate said. "I hope they all rot in hell."

"Those three won't be missed, that's for sure."

Sullivan waited until a freight wagon rumbled past.

"A detective looked into the case," he said. "Three men shot dead at the same time is unusual, even for Five Points."

Kate felt a small stab of panic.

"And what did the detective say?"

"He said it was a professional job, done

by a man who knew how to use a revolver."

"Is that so?" Kate said.

"A man like Ben Hollister," Sullivan said.

"I'm sure it wasn't him," Kate said.

"Well, they dug .31 caliber balls out of the dead men. Hollister killed his last man with a .44. I doubt that he would go up against three violent toughs with a belly gun."

Kate swallowed hard.

"Then who do you suspect, Constable Sullivan?"

"A professional assassin from out of town, I'd say. And the detective agrees."

"I hope you catch your man," Kate said.

"Little chance of that. He's probably back in Chicago by this time."

Sullivan touched his cap.

"Well, it's good news for you, Miss Cotter."

"It is indeed," Kate said.

What Shannon was not able to hide for long was that the attack had left her pregnant and her father finally learned the truth about what had happened.

Filled with impotent rage, Patrick Cotter demanded to know if the police had been informed.

"It's too late for that, Pa," Kate said. "The three men who raped Shannon are dead."

"But who? How?"

"Sam Sullivan says they were shot by a hired assassin. I say it was the wrath of God that brought them to justice."

"Then thanks to the Good Lord that we will soon leave this accursed place," Cotter said.

"And to where?" Shannon said. "Everywhere I go I take this vile belly with me."

"A while ago I wrote to my brother Shamus who resides in the city of Nashville in Tennessee," Patrick said. "I explained our straightened circumstance and" — the man searched for a word, then accepted reality and hung his head — "begged for his help."

"Why didn't you tell me you'd done this?" Kate said.

She stared at her father, half in anger, half in pity.

"I feared that he might refuse," Patrick said.

Kate's face softened and tears glistened in her eyes.

She put her hand on Patrick's shoulder and said, "Pa, what have you done? The Cotters ask charity of no one, not even their kin."

"Well, now it's spilled milk," Patrick said. He reached into the inside pocket of his threadbare coat and produced a folded letter.

"Read this aloud, child, so that Shannon can hear."

Kate took the letter, brushed away a tear and read.

May 9, 1852
Nashville, Tennessee

My Dearest Brother,

It is sorry I am to hear of the travails that beset you and yours.

Of course, you must come to Nashville at once, and to that aim I'm sending you a most singular man by the name of Isaac Kerrigan, a saw doctor by trade.

In the pursuit of his profession, Isaac had traveled extensively and he is well suited to bring the wagon and horses I am providing for you.

His son, Joseph, a stalwart lad who will be of great help to you, will accompany his father.

I am happy to report that the Indian tribes you may encounter, among them the fierce Shawnee, are smoking the peace pipe of late, thanks to the efforts of our brave dragoons.

You and your family face a long, arduous journey. My atlas tell me it is all of seven 'undred miles, but keep the Appalachian Mountains in sight and haste ye to my side.

Your Fond Brother,
Shamus

After Kate finished reading, she said, "Then it's settled."

"I expect the wagon to be here in two weeks or less," Patrick said. "We had best be ready to leave on the instant."

Kate saw her sister's troubled face, the terrible deadness in her eyes that had been there since she was attacked.

"Seven hundred miles of wild Indians, mountains, and river crossings, Shannon," she said. "We must think of it as a great adventure."

"Don't talk to me of adventures," Shannon said. "All I want to do now is die and the sooner the better."

Shannon spat out spiteful words as though eager to get rid of the bad taste they left in her mouth.

Patrick looked like a man who'd just been punched in the gut.

He sprang to his feet and slapped Shannon hard across her cheek.

"How dare you talk of death as we move

to a new life?" he said.

Then, his voice breaking, "I will not stand for it. I will not . . ."

Shocked by the scarlet mark of his hand on Shannon's fair cheek, and appalled at the enormity of what he'd just done, Patrick groaned like a soul in torment and fled to his room.

Kate sat in silence and listened to her sister's bitter sobs.

She had but a small family and now it was slowly breaking apart.

From now on she'd have to be strong and lead the way, keep them together.

It is a dark tunnel you're looking through, Kate Cotter, she told herself. *But you must make sure that there's light at the end of it.*

CHAPTER ELEVEN

Isaac Kerrigan was a good-looking man in his late fifties, but Kate Cotter had eyes only for his handsome son.

Joseph was eighteen years old that spring, a strapping lad with a fine, bold mustache and a thick mane of hair to match. Born in Ireland, he had eyes that were as clear and gray as a Donegal mist and a smile as bright as morning.

For Kate, it was love at first sight.

She knew from the first that was the man she'd marry.

Some say it can't happen like that, but it does and more times than people imagine. When Kate first looked into Joseph Kerrigan's eyes she knew in her heart that she could not go on without him at her side.

He was a man to live her life with, and for Kate, there would be no going back from it, not in a year, or ten, or a hundred.

Apart from difficult river crossings, swollen from the spring melt, and the collapse of a wagon wheel that took two full days to repair, the long trek to Tennessee proved to be uneventful.

Isaac Kerrigan knew the trails and was an excellent hand with horses and he was a good camp cook, a skill he patiently taught Kate.

As Shannon sulked in the back of the wagon along with the supplies and the Cotters' few sticks of furniture, and Patrick grew more silent and withdrawn with each passing day, Kate and Joseph were thrown together and took great delight in each other's company.

Night after night they sat together and watched the smoke rise from the campfire and reach toward the stars.

"One day Kate, I'll grab a handful of those and scatter them in your hair," Joseph once said.

Kate said he was being silly, but secretly she was pleased beyond measure. She'd never met, or had ever hoped to meet, a man who talked such pretties.

It was inevitable that by the time they reached Nashville, they were head over heels in love and desirous of getting married as soon as was possible.

■ ■ ■ ■

Unlike his thin, aesthetic brother, Shamus Cotter was a fat, jolly man full of boisterous good humor, and his eyes were as black and bright as a bird's. He habitually wore a brocade vest, a brown, swallow-tailed coat, and a high hat as shiny as a stovepipe. A trader in Irish horses by profession, he was a notorious rogue and cheerfully acknowledged that fact.

He welcomed the Cotter family warmly, took stock of both Shannon's belly and Kate's beauty but said nothing of the former and praised the latter.

"And I have a place for you to live, Patrick," Shamus said. "It's not a palace but it's a roof over your heads."

"It's beholden I am to you, my brother," Patrick said.

"And there's a clerk's stool reserved for you in me office," Shamus said. "And don't object now, but I'll pay you no less than five dollars a week, less two dollars for rent."

"That is handsome of you, Shamus," Patrick said.

Kate thought it somewhat less than handsome, but then, beggars can't be choosers.

The house was small and rough, the

ground floor of a tenement, but compared to their hovel in Five Points, Kate decided it was a step up, albeit a small one.

There were, at least, narrow windows that could be opened to let in light and fresh air and the house itself was free of the rats and other vermin that had so plagued them in New York, making each day such a misery.

In 1852, Nashville was a growing city with almost twenty thousand inhabitants.

It was still very much a river port town, but did have a single railroad line. Clustered around the rail yard were four machine shops that employed more than four hundred people.

But in Kate's day, most of the city's manufacturers were traditional craftsmen, tinsmiths, carriage builders, and boot and shoemakers.

"Everyone needs a saw doctor," Joseph Kerrigan said, as he and Kate strolled along the bank of the Cumberland River close to the bustling port. "I can make a good living when we're wed."

Kate nodded but said nothing.

"It seems that since we arrived in Nashville two weeks ago you're constantly lost in thought, but I fear not thoughts of me," Joseph said.

"I am thinking of you, Joe," Kate said.

"I'm worried that the secret I hide might harm you, harm us."

The young man smiled.

"And what great secret can you possibly have, Kate?" he frowned. "Unless there's someone else."

"There's no one else, Joe, only you. Now and forever."

"Then tell me, Kate."

The day was warm, bright with sun, the only sound the distant clang and clatter of the dockyard. Jays quarreled in a nearby beech tree and sent down a shower of leaves and twigs. A man walking his dog stopped, and they both stared at a passing flatboat loaded with timber.

"Joe, let us sit under the tree and I'll tell you what is weighing so heavily on me," Kate said.

Once they were both settled and Kate had arranged the skirts of her morning dress, a pale blue hand-me-down from Shamus's wife that fit quite well, for unlike her husband, she was a slender woman.

"Well, then, Kate," Joseph said. "Tell me what's troubling you so. Is it your poor sister's sorry plight?"

"Yes, it is, but more than that."

Joseph Kerrigan waited. An errant breeze tossed a raven's wing of hair over his handsome forehead and he impatiently brushed it back.

"Three men attacked Shannon and —" Kate said.

"I know. Your father told me."

"The names of those men will be branded on my heart forever."

Kate stared up at small white clouds gliding across the sky like lilies on a pond.

"Bill Wooten, Tom Van Meter, and Chauncey Upsell," she said.

She turned and looked into Joseph's eyes.

"Do you wonder that I remember them so well?"

The young man seemed to be at a loss for words, but Kate filled the silence.

"I remember them so well because I killed all three of them. I shot them down in a warehouse stairwell and then spit on them."

Joseph was taken aback and his lean jaw dropped.

"With a gun?" he said.

"No, Joe." She made a barrel of her forefinger. "Bang! I did it with this."

"But . . . but how did you get such a thing as a gun?"

"It was a .31 caliber Colt revolver I borrowed from a friend and have since returned. At close range, it was a good enough weapon."

"And all three are dead?"

"Dead as they're ever going to be."

The young man was quiet for a moment.

Then he said, "Well, Kate, may the devil make a ladder of their backbones when he's picking apples in the gardens of hell."

"Then you do not blame me?"

"Blame you? No, they got what they deserved and I admire you, Kate. What a fine, strong, brave woman you are. It's proud I am that you've accepted me to be your husband, unworthy as I may be."

Joseph kissed Kate on the cheek.

"I will call you *Aoifa,* the Irish warrior princess who slaughtered a hundred Viking warriors in a longhouse to avenge the murder of her liege lord, the noble High King Fergal MacNeil."

"You will do no such thing. You will call me Kate and Mrs. Kerrigan and nothing else."

"Then it will be so and we will never talk of dead men in a stairwell again."

"Up, and then give me your hand, Joe," Kate said. "It will be time for supper soon."

Joseph helped Kate to her feet.

"Joe, I was thinking when we were on the journey from Five Points that I love being outdoors in all kinds of weather, living rough and just making do."

"It's a fine life if a person is cut out for such a thing, Kate."

"Would it not be wonderful if we had land that we could crop and graze and on which raise our children? We'd set store by our kinfolk and when trouble appeared we'd stand against it as a family."

"And fight, by God."

"Yes, we'd fight, you and I, Joe, shoulder to shoulder."

The young man tipped back his head and laughed.

"It is a warrior princess you are, Kate Cotter, and no mistake. But that life is not for us. You'll be a saw doctor's wife and we'll make our home right here in Nashville, not on the wild frontier among wild animals and savages."

"But it's a dream, Joe, is it not?"

"Yes, it is, Kate, but not one to hold on to for overlong."

"One more thing, Joe, before we can wed," Kate said. "I have committed a grievous mortal sin three times over. We can't stand at the altar until I go to confession and a priest has said God has forgiven me."

"Then we must go and talk with Father John MacDonald," Joseph said. "He is not Irish like us, but a Scotsman born to a clan that well understands the ways of revenge.

We will heed his counsel or not, Kate, but either way, it's husband and wife we'll be."

Three weeks later Kate and Joseph Kerrigan were married with the blessings of Holy Mother Church.

It seemed that in the matter of vengeance killings, Father MacDonald was prepared to grant a little leeway.

CHAPTER TWELVE

It was agreed that Kate and her husband should move in with Patrick Cotter until they found a suitable home, Joseph steadfastly refusing any monetary help from his father.

Weeks, then months passed and then, as Kate's first child quickened in her belly, Shannon's baby was born dead. A day later, Shannon lost her battle with life and passed into the darkness she had long considered a blessing.

Patrick Cotter was devastated. The slap he'd given his daughter, never forgotten nor forgiven, racked his conscience, and he withdrew even more into himself. He no longer penned the poems that had earlier prevented him from slipping away into despair.

On a cold, rainy fall morning, Shannon was buried in a dank, deep, and rectangular grave in the cemetery of the local Catholic

Church.

Dressed in black mourning, Kate stood by the graveside and wondered what sin her sister had committed to be born under such a dark star.

The answer was none, of course. A child was born with original sin, washed away at birth, and no other.

As though reading her thoughts, Joseph put his arm around Kate's growing waist and whispered, "She's in a far better place now."

Kate nodded and said, "Surely she could be in no worse."

Her father glanced over at her, his face empty, as though incapable of dealing with the pain that was now inflicted on him.

As the priest finished his prayers for the dead, the sky erupted. Thunder blasted and lightning scrawled across the sky like the signature of a demented god.

The rain grew heavier, and one of the grave diggers, a thin man with a sad, timeless face, said to Joseph, "Perhaps the ladies should withdraw."

The priest, soaked to the skin and late for breakfast, made a sign of the cross above the grave and then hurried into the church.

Kate, her Uncle Shamus, and his wife followed him.

Patrick remained at the graveside as the diggers threw down shovelfuls of dirt that drummed on the coffin lid. He stayed there for an hour and let the rain soak him and the thunder, with little respect for the grieving, bluster and threaten.

Two weeks later he died.

Of pneumonia, the doctor said.

But Kate knew her father had died of a broken heart.

Joseph Kerrigan said a prayer at Patrick's grave side that managed to purge the worst of Kate's grief.

Neither of them knew that a few years later, he, too, would be dead.

CHAPTER THIRTEEN

Now Kate Kerrigan worried over a different Shannon, her frail little girl who ate her rye bread and milk so daintily and smiled as she did so.

Shannon had a cough that came and went and often ran a fever that alarmed Kate.

The child also had night sweats and needed to be seen by a doctor.

But how to pay for one?

Well, she would just have to find a way.

Marry Fin Gannon? The dairyman had plenty of money.

Kate smiled and dismissed the idea.

After Joe, there could be no other man for her.

"Ma, is there any more?" Shannon said, holding her up her empty milk bowl.

Kate fancied that she looked like Mr. Dickens' Oliver Twist.

She poured milk into Shannon's bowl,

then the child said, "Can I have more bread, Ma?"

"Of course you can," Kate said, smiling. "There's plenty."

But of course there was not.

Kate gave her daughter her own meager portion and didn't think twice about it.

Across town, an hour's walk away, Kate's oldest son Trace worked in a store that had a carved wooden sign hanging above the door that proudly proclaimed:

ARTHUR LUNDY
GUNSMITH
Shotgun repairs a specialty

Picture a kindly old craftsman with spectacles perched at the end of his nose, a white beard, and twinkling blue eyes . . . and you don't have Arthur Lundy.

He was a cantankerous, cranky, old curmudgeon who hated children, dogs, and humanity in general and went out of his way to stamp on wildflowers. His thin nose was curved like a hook, his blue eyes were flinty and avaricious, and his skin was the color of wood ash.

Lundy talked little and after every utterance his thin mouth snapped shut again like a steel purse.

Yet, for some reason known only to himself and God, he liked young Trace Kerrigan.

Lundy had been going through hard times since the war ended but not from a lack of quality in his work. No better gunsmith could be found for two hundred miles in any direction.

The excellence of his craftsmanship had helped see Lundy through the war years, when he had labored hard for the Confederacy, repairing battle-damaged weapons, and converting old flintlock rifles and muskets, still abundant in the South, into more modern and effective percussion cap weapons.

"I helped keep the South shooting," he once told Trace. "Kept us in the fight. Why, Jefferson Davis his ownself sat right where you're sitting and said, 'Thank'ee kindly, Mr. Lundy, for all your efforts. When this war ends in victory for the Confederate States of America I'll personally pin a gold medal on your chest.' "

The war ended in defeat and Lundy never got his medal. To make matters worse, the Yankees didn't care for him that much.

Arthur Lundy was sixty-eight years old when Trace first went to work for him, but looked many years older. His shoulders, stooped from years working bent over on gun actions, were as curved as an old dowager at her knitting. His eyesight was failing and arthritis caused walnut-sized knuckles on both hands.

Trace Kerrigan had a love for all things mechanical, but once introduced to the sculpture in steel that was a fine rifle, he wished to be nothing else but a gunsmith.

"Remember this, Trace," Lundy told him. "All a man needs for happiness is a good gun, a good horse, and a good wife. You can do without the last, but hang on to the other two."

Lundy took on Trace as an informal paid apprentice . . . paid sporadically, anyway. A dozen times in the past seven months, Lundy was forced to ask Trace to allow him to record what he was owed in a ledger, to be paid when things improved.

"Hard times coming down, Trace," he'd say. "We have to tighten our belts, boy."

But those occasions brought hardship to the Kerrigan family.

Trace kept almost none of the meager pay he received and passed the bulk of it on to his widowed mother to help with the care of the children.

He had the Kerrigan pride and never let

Lundy see the disappointment he felt at those times when the old gunsmith had not earned the money to pay him.

But the privation cut deep and his mother felt it more keenly that anyone, though she never let it show in front of the youngsters.

One aspect of his job, though, infuriated Trace.

It had nothing to do with old Lundy himself, who was honest in his way, but with Lundy's son, Alec, a mean-looking youth with the cold, calculating eyes of a carrion-eater.

Alec was a chronic drinker and when his father was out, Trace had caught him more than once dipping his hand into the gun shop cashbox to steal whiskey money.

The stolen dollars took the bread out of the mouths of the Kerrigan family and Trace's dislike for the young man grew.

Now, on the morning that Fin Gannon dunned his mother for milk money and on a week that Trace had gone into the ledger, Alec Lundy looked up from the cashbox, saw the apprentice's eyes on him and sneered.

"You keep your damned mouth shut, you Irish brat. I'm only taking my due."

"You're stealing, Alec," Trace said.

"Yes, and it's none of your damned business."

"Put the money back," Trace said.

Alec was already half-drunk and his fists bunched.

He took a step closer to Trace and said, "Suppose I shut your mouth for you?"

Alec was thirty years old, not as tall as Trace, but he outweighed him by thirty pounds, all of it in his chest and shoulders.

It was rumored that Alec had once beaten a man so badly he'd almost died, and old Arthur had to pay a considerable amount of money to smooth things over.

"Suppose you step over here and try to shut my mouth," Trace said.

By comparison with Lundy, Trace Kerrigan was slender, but every ounce of him was hard bone and whipcord muscle. He was young, tough with quick hands and a fighting heart.

He'd learned his fistfighting in the hard school of the Five Points streets and though many tried, none of the boys of his age, and older, had ever cut him down to size.

Now Trace faced up to a much bigger opponent, but had met guys like Alec before.

Alec Lundy welcomed the fight.

His face was livid with anger and his eyes

glittered with the savage lust to smash and destroy.

His lips bared back from yellow, prominent teeth, he said, "I'll beat the Irish pig stink out of you, boyo."

Lundy was big boned and weighed two hundred pounds. He was full of raw power, untrained but brutal.

Trace was set, his fists up and ready, but Lundy's right hand hardly traveled six inches before it crashed into Trace's chin and set him reeling across the room as his flailing feet fought for balance.

Trace's back crashed into the front door as he fell and set its bell jangling.

Grinning, Lundy was on him in a flash.

The man's booted foot crashed into Trace's left side, trying to break ribs and drive them into his lungs.

Gasping from pain, Trace rolled away from a second kick, grabbed the top of a workbench and dragged himself to his feet.

Fireworks exploding in his head, Trace sucked air into his lungs and pain spiked at him with every tormented breath.

Then Lundy came at him again.

But slowly this time, his eager grin anticipating the kill.

Trace moved away from Lundy's first punch and jabbed a hard straight right into the man's mouth, splitting his bottom lip wide open.

Lundy took a wary step back and his eyes were wild, as though the taste of his own blood shocked him.

Trace slipped a wild, looping right and hammered two quick punches into Lundy's face. Lundy staggered back a step and Trace hit him again with a driving uppercut that slammed into the man's chin and snapped his head back.

Lundy went down on one knee, spitting blood and a tooth. He groaned and his open hand went up in a gesture of surrender.

But there was no mercy in Trace.

Five Points had taught him how to fight to win, not to prove himself a gentleman and allow an opponent to rise who was still capable of fight.

Trace hit Lundy hard with a right hand hook that crashed into the side of Lundy's face with the sound of a sledgehammer hitting a hollow log.

This time the man fell on his right side and then rolled over onto his belly. He tried to push up with his hands, but Lundy was done. He collapsed onto his belly again and lay still.

Trace knew the fight was over and he'd won.

He dropped his hands and at that moment the door chimed open and Arthur Lundy stepped inside.

The old man took in at a glance what had happened.

His son was groaning on the floor, his face covered in blood, and Trace's face was swollen, his shirt torn, and his knuckles scraped.

"Get back to work, Trace," he said.

Alec Lundy heard his father's voice and stumbled to his feet.

He cast a glaring, hate-filled eye on Trace then lurched to the door.

"Alec, come back," Arthur said. "We must talk, son."

"We've nothing to talk about, old man," Alec said.

He threw open the door and vanished into the street.

CHAPTER FOURTEEN

"And then what happened?" Kate Kerrigan said, dabbing something that stung on Trace's swollen eye.

Shannon sat on her mother's lap and Ivy and Niall stared at Trace with fascinated, hero-worshipping eyes as he told his story.

Quinn had not yet returned home from his job at a private library.

"Well, after the fight I worked for a while, but Mr. Lundy didn't speak to me. He seemed very upset, but with me or Alec or both of us I couldn't say. Finally I walked back to the old man's workbench and said to him, 'Mr. Lundy, I see you're still working on the Colt revolver.' Now I expected to be rebuffed, but to my surprise he smiled at me."

"So he wasn't mad at you, Trace," Ivy said.

"No, I guess not. Mr. Lundy had been piecing together good parts from several scrapped Colts for weeks now, fitting and grinding and polishing to create a customized revolver he said would be unlike any other in the world, a gun as fine as any could be."

"And was it?" Kate said.

"I'm coming to that, Ma."

Trace gingerly fingered the swelling on his eye and winced.

"Poor Trace," Ivy said.

"Now I supposed that Mr. Lundy was gunsmithing the Colt to give himself a reward for his lifetime of hard work, and a compensation for some of the difficulties he had to endure these days. I did not blame him at all. The old man, alone in the world except for a drunkard son who showed no love for him, deserved something good."

"And so he did, I suppose," Kate said. "But just wait until I see that no-good Alec Lundy. He'll rue the day he was born, I swear you that."

"No, Ma," Trace said. "I gave him a terrible beating and we'll let it go at that."

"But he harmed one of mine," Kate said.

"And paid for it," Trace said.

"Well, if you say so, Trace," Kate said. "But I'd still like to take a stick to him."

"And what about the gun, Trace?" Niall said, his young face eager.

"Well, Mr. Lundy said the revolver was

finished and he'd just put the final touches to the polishing. Says he, 'All I did today was to make this Colt look the best it can when I present it to you.' "

"Now I was struck silent — surely I'd misheard. But Mr. Lundy saw my confusion and said, 'Yes, Trace. I've not smithed this revolver for myself, but for you.' "

" 'Sir . . . but . . . why?' I said. 'I have done nothing to deserve such a fine thing!' "

"Indeed you have, Trace," Kate said. "Up at five every morning, rain or shine, to go work in his slave shop, and him not paying you half the time. Don't sell yourself short, son."

Trace smiled at that and said, " 'You've been the brightest light in a life growing steadily darker,' Mr. Lundy said. 'You've worked faithfully and worked hard, and in seven months you have learned more of the gunsmith's art than many manage in seven years.' "

"No more praise than you deserve, Trace," Kate said. "The old skinflint."

"Well, Ma, he did say that I'd patiently endured even when he was unable to pay me. 'Even now I cannot pay you,' he said. 'Not your back wages nor your current wages. Money has constantly gone missing from the cashbox, and I can't make it up again.' "

" 'Because that drunken son of yours has taken it all,' you should have told him," Kate said.

"Ma, I was honest with Mr. Lundy and I did tell him that the Colt revolver was surely worth more than I was owed. But he said if he could double its value, triple it, he'd gladly give it to me and consider himself on the better end of the bargain.

" 'Then I don't have the words, sir,' I said. And says he, 'Has that fine mother of yours not taught you the value of a simple, Thank you? That's all that is needed.' "

"Well, let's see it, Trace," Niall said.

Trace reached into the oily, burlap sack at his feet and produced the revolver.

"Is it not a beauty?" he said.

The modified .36-caliber revolver possessed a balance unlike any other Trace had held. He lifted the empty weapon and sighted down its gleaming barrel, noting how easy it was to maintain a steady hand and light-but-firm squeeze on the polished wooden grip.

He was unsure of all that the gunsmith had done to perfect the revolver's balance, but the work would have impressed Sam'l Colt himself.

Its appearance was substantially that of a

Colt 1861 Navy, the type of revolver upon whose frame Lundy's modifications had skillfully been added.

"Mr. Lundy told me the gun will aim and shoot like the glory of God," Trace said.

"Trace, please don't take the name of our Creator in vain," Kate said.

Her son grinned.

"Ma, you're not familiar with guns. If you were, you'd know what Mr. Lundy meant."

Trace held the Colt out to Kate.

"Do you want to hold it? Don't worry, it's not loaded, but be careful not to drop it on your toe."

"I can see from here that it's a finely crafted weapon," Kate said.

"But you must test the action, Ma. Feel how silky smooth it is."

"I'll take your word for it, Trace," Kate said.

She remembered another Colt in another place and time.

Shannon . . . Ben Hollister . . . the flash and bang of a gun in the dark . . . the faces of dying men . . . the urge to kill and kill again . . .

"It's a fine revolver, Trace," Kate said, blinking away visions. "And please tell Mr. Lundy that I said so."

Chapter Fifteen

"My mother presents her compliments and says the revolver you built for me is a fine gun," Trace said. "She's not much used to firearms but seemed to appreciate the workmanship."

"I hope it will give you much good use, and protection, and enjoyment," Lundy said.

"Thank you, sir. Again."

"Enough, I grow weary of thanks. But there is one thing. Don't speak of this to Alec. I know that he anticipated being the owner of the Colt. He will not be happy to know you have it."

"I will say nothing about it to him, Mr. Lundy. I seek no more trouble with your son."

"There's no point in me putting a false face on it. Alec does not like you. He sees in you all the things he is not. You're young, strong, handsome as the devil himself, and above all talented. I have tried to teach Alec my craft, and he has faltered and fumbled and failed."

"Perhaps with time . . ." Trace said.

"There is no more time. Though he is my own son, my flesh and blood, his manner and rudeness and lack of character offends me. I celebrate in my heart every time he leaves this place and I can do my work without having to endure him."

"I'm sorry things are like that with you," Trace said. "Him being your son and all. Will it cause you to be angry with me if I confess to you that I don't like to be around Alec, either?"

The old man's smile was as cold as frost on a tree limb.

"It would surprise me to hear anything else," Lundy said. "He treats you with much contempt and meanness. I see him and his ways more clearly than he realizes."

It was pure impulse, not thought out, but Trace decided to tell his employer what he knew about Alec's theft from the shop and how he'd confronted him. As soon as the words were out he wondered if he'd done the right thing to speak.

Lundy looked at him with no change of expression.

"You're telling me nothing I didn't know,

Trace. I saw Alec in the act of theft not two weeks back with my own eyes. So drunk was he that he didn't realize I had seen him. Does he think me such a dolt, that he can help himself to the meager profits of this enterprise and think I will never realize it?"

The old man stared out the dusty window into the busy street, the expression on his wrinkled face both sad and angry.

"Damn! There are times I hate him, as I know he hates me!"

He turned to Trace again.

"Is it a sin, a great sin, for a father to hate his own son?

"I don't know, Trace said. "Tonight I will ask my mother. Sometimes she has answers for such questions."

Until that moment, Trace had not realized the depth of antipathy between father and son and how deep and black went their hatreds.

Lundy came to his feet and paced stiffly about, looking distraught.

"Trace, tell, me why it must be this way. A man's only son, born of his loins, yet nothing comes of it but sorrow and loathing. I wanted a son who would make a father proud, a boy who would grow strong and straight and be a man of honor. And look what I sired, Trace. A thief, a liar, a drunkard, a whoremonger, and a fool."

"Mr. Lundy, I'm just a young sprout and I have little knowledge of the world, but I beseech you not to utter words you'll later wish you hadn't. My father always said to remember that words unleashed from the lips can never be reclaimed again."

It felt odd to Trace, a callow youth giving counsel to a man decades his senior.

Lundy muttered a few profane words beneath his breath.

He turned to a seldom-used desk in the corner of the room and from a drawer produced a brass flask embossed with scenes of some desperate naval battle.

The old man pulled the stopper and hefted the flask to his lips.

"Half gone, by God. He's stolen even my whiskey, and good bonded bourbon it was."

Lundy lifted the flask and drained it dry.

Trace was deeply disturbed.

He'd seldom seen Arthur Lundy drink, and never had he seen him display such raw emotion.

It made him realize just how fortunate he was to come from a family that, despite a world of troubles, managed to make its way through life without any fighting beyond the usual day-to-day disputes and quarrels that came along with simply being kin.

"Damn him to hell!" Lundy bellowed.

He threw the empty flask so hard against the brick wall it clattered, dented, onto the floor among the dust, grit, waste lead and metal shavings common to all gunsmith shops.

Trace urged Lundy toward his chair again and desperately tried to calm him down.

But the old man wheeled and faced him with a wild and glaring eye. Lundy lifted a trembling forefinger and aimed it at Trace.

"Do you know what I wanted, Trace? Do you know what I hoped for from the first moment I learned I had a son? Answer me, damn you, do you know?"

Alarmed, Trace shook his head but said nothing.

"I wanted you! From the very moment Alec came into the world I wanted Trace Kerrigan. But what did I get? Tell me what I got? It's obvious to the world, so why not to you? Tell me. Tell me."

Lundy's eyes were frantic, shot through with crooked scarlet veins.

"Mr. Lundy . . ." Trace began, but the words wouldn't come.

"I'll tell you what I got . . . I got trash. Yes, Trace, trash I named Alec and learned to despise more with each passing year, as he has come to despise me."

Lundy finally sat in the chair, spent.

"When Alec was grown he showed his true colors. Oh, but they were dark colors, dark as the lowest pit of hell. No wonder I welcomed you so happily into this place! You were what I had wanted all along, not the wastrel hellhound I was given."

Lundy looked at Trace with dead eyes.

"Alec will kill me one day," the old man said. "That's how it will end. It's the only way it can end."

Trace had long known the relationship between Lundy the father and Lundy the son was not a good one, but he'd never fully realized until now how deep and dangerous their mutual hatred had become.

He took a knee beside the old man.

"Perhaps if you and Alec lived apart for a while and let old wounds heal? Perhaps —"

"Trace, some wounds can never heal and that's the truth of it," Lundy said.

He motioned to his desk, dusty and little used.

"In there, second drawer, there's another bottle, unless Alec has emptied it as well. Fetch it here to me."

The bottle was half-full of whiskey. Trace did as he was told and handed it to his pathetic employer. He wished Alec had emptied or taken this bottle, too, so old

Lundy couldn't hurt himself with its contents.

The gunsmith put the bottle to his lips and slugged down the raw whiskey, bottled in a slum saloon, then wiped his mouth with the back of his hand.

"You want some, boy?"

"No, sir. Thank you."

"Huh! You know, I forget how young you are sometimes. You have the look of an older young man about you. You could pass for twenty, no lie told."

"I've been told that often, sir."

"Stay away from strong drink and you'll always look years younger," Lundy said. "That's a fact."

The old man drank again. A little color tinged the cheekbones of his ashen face.

"I was speaking to a cattle broker the other day, a Texan by the name of Harry Cribbs. Ever hear tell of him?"

Trace Kerrigan shook his head.

"Well, he was speaking about Alec but I think his words more apply to you. After my discussion with Cribbs, you know what a young and able fellow like you should do, or at least give it some consideration?"

"No, sir, I don't."

"Hear me, then. I would turn my eyes west, and go out to the vast plains and learn the cattle trade. Mark my words, it's cattle that will build many an empire out beyond America's great river."

"My mother has often said that such would be a fine life for the Kerrigan family," Trace said.

"A wise woman is Kate Kerrigan," Lundy said. "Cribbs, a man I don't like, but I listened to him because what he says makes sense. He said the North needs beef to keep the populations of their vast cities fed. Texas can supply that beef, and many a cattle rancher will make millions out of filling Yankee bellies."

Trace let his interest show and Lundy was happy to continue.

"Cribbs says that countless numbers of longhorn Texas cattle were left to roam as free as wild beasts during the war years, and have bred themselves into vast herds that cover the plains as far as a man can see. Any man with courage and determination can build and brand his own herd. With the railroads expanding day by day and cattle to be had for the taking, think what an able young fellow like you could do for himself, Trace."

"It is a thought, Mr. Lundy," Trace said.

"Thinking about a thing never made it so," the old man said. "Go to Texas and you can become a cattleman of means and influence, a man who means something, who is somebody . . . not just a waste like some old gunsmith in a back-alley shop, with a worthless son as his only legacy."

Trace might have spoken up and countered the old man's self-deprecating words, but he was taken by what Lundy had just said about the possibilities looming in Texas cattle.

He'd heard others say similar things, and the thought of heading into that great and opening land and forging a life there resonated in his very soul.

Yes. That could be the future for Trace Kerrigan.

Lundy said, "Now why don't you take that fine revolver out back to the range and fire it a little? Get used to how it feels to shoot, because that's the belt gun you'll take to Texas."

"You don't mind me doing that even though I'm here to work?"

"Holy martyrs, didn't you just hear me suggesting it? A gun is little good to a man who doesn't know how to use it well. Load it light to spare what powder you can, but spend some time with it. Learn to shoot it as a fighting revolver should be shot."

"I will, then, straightaway."

After gathering paper cartridges, Trace headed out back to the enclosed rear lot, where a row of stout painted-circle targets was in place, up against a fence built from squared lumber so thick no ball could penetrate and do harm to others.

The shooting range was there primarily for the benefit of customers who wanted to test-fire their prospective purchases. There were no customers at the moment, though, so Trace had an excellent opportunity to test out the customized Colt, and set about it at once.

"Well, lad, what think you of it?" Lundy said.

Trace was so intent on aiming his new gun at the target that he had not heard Lundy exit into the rear lot and come up behind him.

Trace jumped at the sound of Lundy's voice, and fired a wild shot that thudded into the heavy rearward fence two feet to the right of the target.

"Well! We'll put that one down to me startling you," Lundy said. "I see from the other prior bullet holes that you'd done better before I came out here."

"The Colt is a dream to shoot," Trace said. "That balance is perfect, it feels good in the hand, and it shoots to the point of aim.

"Except for that last one, I'd say."

"Make fun if you want," Trace said, "but watch this first." He aimed again, carefully, and fired a shot dead center into the bull's-eye.

"Your point is made," Lundy said. "And it gladdens my heart to see you taking so well to my masterpiece."

"It's the best gift ever given to me," Trace said.

"And damn you, it should be mine, and I'm taking it back."

CHAPTER SIXTEEN

The voice came from behind Arthur Lundy, from the rear shop doorway. Trace and the old man both knew at once whom it belonged to.

"That ain't his gun," Alec said.

He was already drunk though the sky was only just beginning to lose the light of day.

"I've had my eye on that gun all the time you worked on it, and it's me who will have it! I'm your son, not this damned Mick!"

Arthur, who had been drinking heavily since Trace retrieved the bottle for him, was in no mood to monitor his tongue.

He lifted a hand and waved it dismissively at Alec, as though to wave him back into the gun shop.

"Go sleep it off," the old man said. "You're drunk."

Alec swore and quickly stepped toward his father, and for the first time in their lives the strains between them brought about physical violence.

Alec backhanded the old man, a calculated, vicious blow that cracked like a gunshot.

The old man staggered and fell, his jaw hanging at a strange angle.

Trace was so stunned he froze, not even daring to breathe.

Alec glanced at his unconscious father, mumbled alcohol-slurred words Trace could not understand, then slowly turned his head.

"Give me my gun," he said. "I will have need for it."

He stepped toward Trace, his eyes ugly.

The words roused Trace out of his stupor and he took a step back.

It took a moment before he remembered he was armed.

As Alec advanced another step clarity broke through and Trace acted.

He lifted the Colt and pointed it directly at the other man's chest.

"Is this what you want?" he said. He raised the muzzle of the revolver for emphasis. "Maybe I should give it to you lead first."

Alec laughed, an ugly, reckless sound.

"Don't be a damned fool. You don't have the guts to pull the trigger on a man."

Staggering drunk as he was, he lunged and

managed to get his hand on the gun. Stunned with surprise, Trace froze again, and Alec jerked the gun from his hand.

He didn't take possession of it, though.

The revolver's barrel was still hot from Trace's target practice and Alec yelped and let it drop to the ground.

The gun landed in the middle of the firing range ground.

Younger and impaired only by fear and the tension of the moment, Trace went after the gun first.

Alec tripped him, though, and moments later had the weapon in his possession again. He leveled it shakily in Trace's direction as Trace came deftly back to his feet.

Trace yelled his anger and rushed at the older man.

Alec pulled the trigger.

CLICK.

The hammer snapped but no shot came. Trace had emptied the chambers during his practice shooting, though in the heat of the moment he had been as unaware of it as Alec had.

Trace stepped close and his fist connected hard with Alec's chin.

The man jolted backward and landed on his rump, and Trace danced over him, gripping his right hand and fearing he might have broken his finger against Alec's sharp chin bone.

Alec got up, roaring in fury and rubbing his jaw, clutching the empty gun tightly in his hand. Trace made a grab for it but missed. Alec, roaring again, swung the revolver against Trace's temple and knocked him cold in a lucky blow.

For a moment there was silence in the enclosed back lot.

Alec stood slump-shouldered, Trace senseless at his feet, his father groaning and beginning to move slightly a few yards away. Alec, alcohol coursing through his bloodstream and his heart beating over-fast against his ribs, tried to clear his mind by force of will, and assess his situation.

Trace Kerrigan was so still that Alec thought he was dead, until he saw the faint movement of respiration.

Turning to look back at his father, his eye was drawn to the edge of the firing range, where Trace had placed a supply of ammunition for his shooting practice.

Alec chuckled and soon had the Colt reloaded despite his fumbling fingers. Re-armed, he felt a surge of victory in knowing he now had the advantage. Let the boy rush him now — he'd be greeted by a bullet.

Trace, though, would rush no one.

He remained unconscious at Alec's feet, head laid back and eyes closed almost completely, though enough of a slit remained to reveal the lower whites of his eyes, showing his eyes were rolled upward in their sockets.

Alec, considering his next move, pulled a flask from his pocket and took a swig. So drunk was he already that the influx of a new jolt of alcohol was almost enough to drop him where he stood.

He capped and pocketed the flask, and found himself pondering the option of putting a bullet through the brain of Trace Kerrigan while he lay helpless. He could place the gun in the hand of his still unconscious father and leave him to deal with the consequences of the murder.

He'd despised Trace Kerrigan since the first day he'd come to work at the gun shop. For seven months he'd had the growing awareness that his father possessed a far greater liking for the young man than for his own son . . . and it infuriated Alec.

He'd never gotten to the point of trying to rid himself of young Kerrigan, but then, no tempting situation like the one now at hand had previously presented itself. Nor had a development as infuriating as his father's gift of the custom Colt to Kerrigan.

He could do away with the pest, and leave his father to bear the brunt. Punish them both.

The tiny spark of moral consciousness that still flickered in Alec Lundy's soul put up only the feeblest resistance to that idea. Liquor had taken away from him any meaningful sense of restraint.

Arthur Lundy carried with him at all times a small revolver, tucked away in a side holster. That fact was about to become a crucial factor in the life of Trace Kerrigan.

The gunsmith had been slowly coming around after being knocked unconscious by the backhand blow delivered by his son.

He rolled over, the movement shooting pain through his broken jaw. His vision slowly cleared, and what he saw from his prone position was at first hard to make out, then hard to believe.

Alec was standing over a seemingly senseless Trace Kerrigan, aiming the customized Colt at him. Alec's stance was that of a man clearly about to shoot . . . but he was wavering. Through drunkenness, perhaps, or indecision about where to put the bullet, or maybe whether to shoot at all.

Moving sluggishly despite a sense of desperation as he comprehended the situation, Arthur rolled to one side and reached beneath his jacket flap to find his revolver, and in his distraction Alec did not notice his father's movement.

He decided at last that he would shoot the boy in the chest, and that, yes indeed, he did have it in him to really do it.

Then he would put the Colt into the hand of his father and be gone. Who could say? Maybe the old gunsmith himself would actually believe he had been the one who killed his young employee, by accident or some unremembered intention.

It would hardly matter . . . the local constabulary would certainly believe Arthur was the killer. No one left alive, except Arthur himself, would know that Alec had even been present.

"Alec."

The voice made the drunken man start and step to the side, turning in a wheeling stagger to see who had spoken.

He was stunned to see his father on his feet. He was unsteady but standing, and in his hand was the small revolver he carried, but which Alec had forgotten about in the wild drunken race of events.

"Pa," Alec said, and steadied himself, facing the old man.

"I can't let you do that, boy," Arthur said. "I've stood by and watched you become a liar and a drunkard, but I'll not allow you to put the stain of murder on your soul."

"Murder . . . I ain't murdered nobody, Pa. He's just knocked cold, that's all."

"I saw what you were about to do, boy. I won't let it happen. I'll drop you where you stand before I allow it."

"Pa, don't talk that way! It's me, it's your son, Alec!"

"I'll not allow my son kill a good lad, or go to face judgment in this world or the next as a murderer. If I have to do it, shoot you I will, Alec."

Alec struggled for words and found none. In fact, he couldn't even find his voice. All that came out were strained vocalizations, and behind them a fury of spirit that washed away the last remnant of common sense and self-control.

He roared like the madman he very nearly was, and he aimed the coveted Colt at Trace Kerrigan's heart.

But the killing shot came from the old man's gun, striking Alec high on his head, cutting a burning pathway through hair and scalp.

Arthur Lundy stood with his smoking revolver in his trembling hand, and watched his son collapse, blood trickling down his face in thin, scarlet fingers.

The Colt dropped from Alec's hand as he went down, and he tumbled on top of it.

Arthur stumbled over to where Alec lay beside Trace Kerrigan, who was beginning to murmur now, and move, coming around to the world of the living again with his pistol-whipped temple throbbing terribly.

The old man hardly noticed Trace, his attention being on the son who had given him so little to be proud of.

"Alec, boy," he said as his son lay supine at his feet. "I didn't want to do it! I had to, boy — you gave me no choice! But I'm sorry for it, son. Sorry indeed."

He looked skyward, tears streaming down. "I've killed my own flesh and blood," he mourned to himself and to the sky. "I've destroyed my own child . . . and surely my own soul."

Arthur went to his knees and laid trembling hands on his son's chest, praying and weeping without any degree of hope.

And then, a realization . . . Alec was still breathing. Faintly, but breathing. And when Arthur pulled back up and looked at his son's face, he saw the eyes flutter.

"I didn't do it after all!" Arthur whispered. "God be praised, he's still breathing!"

CHAPTER SEVENTEEN

The bullet had plowed along the top of Alec's head, digging a shockingly deep furrow in his skull, but the wound was not fatal.

Arthur Lundy always had tended to shoot high with a revolver. An inch or so lower and the bullet would have punched straight into Alec's brain. But for the moment, at least, his son still lived, wounded but not mortally so.

"Come back to me, son! Wake up and speak to me . . . I'm sorry about it all . . ."

A faint groan rose from the throat of Alec Lundy and filled his father with a rising hope, and a realization that perhaps he hadn't despised his son as much as he'd thought. How could a man actually hate the fruit of his own loins, after all?

"Wake up, son. Your father is here. Wake up and we'll get you help. We'll get you patched and let you heal, and it will all be good again."

If Arthur expected his son to come around at all, he anticipated it would be like a slow rise through murky water. He was unprepared for it when Alec's body arched backward and a shuddering spasm passed through him from head to toe and evoked an involuntary loud grunt from Alec's throat. Then his eyes opened, but seemed unable to focus.

"Son? Son! It's all right, boy. You're hurt, but you're alive."

Alec managed to make his eyes lock together for half a moment on his father's face. "Pa? What . . ."

"You're shot, boy. Across the top of your head. Do you not remember?"

"Shot . . ." Alec's eyes fluttered out of focus again. "Shot . . ." And then he did remember.

"You . . . you shot me, Pa."

Arthur had hoped that, somehow, the details of the shooting would have gone unremembered. He looked into his son's blood-covered face and his lip trembled.

"It was . . . it was an accident, Alec. I was trying to scare you so you wouldn't . . . so you wouldn't commit a murder and kill young Trace. You were about to do that. I couldn't let you do such a thing, so I tried to . . . just to scare you, that's all."

"Shot me . . . God, my head . . ."

"It's just a flesh wound, son. Right now it's a bleeding mess, but it will heal."

"You shot me!" Alec said again, as if trying to believe it. His speech, before a muddy garble, was a bit clearer, though his drunken slur lingered. "Shot by my own father . . ."

Arthur hung his head and wept over his supine, bleeding offspring, feeling himself the greatest of all sinners.

Alec groaned and closed his eyes, his head hurting badly now. Though he could not see it for himself, the flow of blood from his furrowed wound onto the earth beneath him was slowing.

He drifted out of awareness for a time he could not determine. When he opened his eyes again he was looking into a moon so bright he had to squint against the light a few moments. As his vision adjusted he was able to see that the stars were bright as well in a velvet-black sky.

He felt stronger. His head still hurt and he was weak, but lying on his back on firm ground, he could not tell if he was dizzy or not.

Arthur still leaned over him, though his weeping had given way to quietness. He looked at his son's bloodied face in the moonlight, and said, "I'm mighty sorry I shot you, boy."

Alec closed his eyes again and said nothing. For half a minute, quiet reigned in the back lot shooting range.

"I'm going to go get a wet cloth to clean your face, Alec," the old man said, pushing to his feet. He turned and strode back toward the rear of the gun shop.

Off to the side, and for the moment forgotten, Trace Kerrigan lay in lingering unconsciousness, unmoving but breathing steadily and quietly, like one asleep.

A few moments later, Alec defied the pain in his head and his sense of weakness to make an attempt to rise.

He was growing more uncomfortable where he lay, something pressing painfully into his back beneath him.

He actually managed to rise, and more surprisingly, keep on his feet.

Slowly he straightened, enjoying the feel of a cool breeze against his crusted face. As he lifted his head to let it breathe over him, though, his head filled with agony, the ditch plowed across his head suddenly pulsing with heightened misery.

I'm shot, he thought. *I've never been shot before . . . always wondered how it would feel. Now I know.*

Shot. By my father.

Lowering his head in an effort to lessen the agony, he saw what he'd been lying on. The gleaming .36-caliber Colt his father had given to that young Kerrigan boy, as if an outsider deserved such a prize gift over Arthur's own son.

It filled Alec with such fury that it made his head surge with pain another time.

He stooped slowly, painfully, and picked up the gun. His now. He would not relinquish or lose it.

His father had gone off, he remembered, to wet a cloth with which to cleanse and cool his brow and face . . . but where was he? He had not returned.

"Is he inside drinking?" Alec muttered. "In there drinking whiskey and leaving me out here to suffer by myself. Damn him! Damn him to hell!"

Still forgetful of the fact that another person also was in the back lot, Alec yielded to irrational fury stoked by physical pain and long-standing familial hatred, and walked with the Colt in hand toward the same door through which his father had disappeared earlier.

Out on the ground of the shooting range, Trace Kerrigan moaned softly and stirred a little, beginning to regain awareness.

Alec heard nothing of it. He entered the

rear door of the gun shop with the Colt dangling in his hand. It was dark inside and Alec stumbled a bit as he felt his way along.

"Pa? Where are you?"

It hurt to shout, he discovered, so he lowered his voice. He smelled a whiff of whiskey.

"You in here drinking, Pa? 'Cause you and me have something to settle. You shot me, Pa, and that ain't something I can sweep out of my mind like dirt off a wood floor. Where are you, Pa?"

The loud clunk of a bottle onto the ground in a front corner let him know where Arthur was, and also that he'd been right . . . the old gunsmith was into his liquor again.

"Pa, I hear you, so you can quit hiding in the dark now. We got some talking to do, you and me."

"I'm mighty sorry, son," the old man said from the darkness. "Nothing has gone the way I wanted. I had no notion of shooting you, but you were ready to kill young Trace, and that would have been wrong. I couldn't let you do it, so I shot. I just stopped you from making a big mistake, and doing something that would have put you on the gallows. I didn't kill you, though, boy, remember that."

"You tried, Pa, you tried. You and I both

know that. And you may have killed me yet — my head hurts like hellfire. You nigh put lead through my brain."

"Forgive me, son. I ask that of you."

Visible to Arthur only by the feeblest ghost-glimmer of light from the street outside, Alec's face grimaced in a sudden charge of pain. He lifted his empty hand to gently touch the side of his head, careful not to let his fingers drift up and over into the throbbing wound itself.

"Dear God, Pa, it hurts! It hurts bad!"

"I'm sorry, son."

"That don't help, Pa. Damn you, it don't help one bit."

He raised the Colt and fired into the corner where his father stood. Alec listened to the man yelp and fall, a dead-weight thud that shook the rough wood floor. The bottle from which Arthur had been drinking clattered on the planks and rolled over to rest against Alec's ankle.

Realizing what he'd just done, he let the Colt drop from his numbed fingers.

It hit the whiskey bottle and shattered it, scattering glass shards and liquor over the floor.

Alec suddenly felt the compulsion to flee.

He lurched toward the front door, opened it, and closed it behind him. The street was mostly darkness.

Stricken by sudden dizziness, Alec tried to descend the three steps that led from the porch down to the street. His feet tangled against each other and he fell, hard, his wounded head slamming into the hard-packed ground.

He was out cold in an instant. Thus he was unable to know, and therefore react, when a heavy freight wagon, laden with lumber, came rumbling fast around the nearest corner, its young driver late in returning to his employer's yard for the night and trying to make up for lost time.

The two dray horses pulling the wagon passed over Alec's unmoving form without touching it.

The steel-rimmed wheels did not.

One passed directly over Alec's neck, snapping gullet and airway and spine, ending his life instantly.

The nineteen-year-old driver, who knew he'd run over *something,* persuaded himself it was merely some unfortunate dog, and hurried on without daring to investigate.

Around the next turn of the street, he began to whistle and force up a feigned cheerfulness, but the effort faltered. "Just a dog," he said to himself. "Just a damned sorry old dog, that's all it was." He drove on.

Seven minutes later, the door to the gun shop opened again and another figure emerged.

Trace Kerrigan, himself nearly as unsteady on his feet as Alec had been because of the concussive blow he'd suffered from being pistol whipped into unconsciousness, looked less like a boy of fifteen than he did a drunk.

The fact that he held in his hand a fine Colt revolver his foot had discovered as he walked through the dark shop made him look dangerous, as well.

The woman who saw him, and then the still form of Alec's corpse in the street, sounded an alarm with a loud shriek that drew the attention of some men loitering in an alley beside a dance hall nearby. They came running and heard what she had to say.

"Which way did he go?" one asked.

"He went down that alley yonder," she said, pointing with a trembling hand. "He had a pistol in his hand."

Two men went up the same alley, looking for the fugitive. Two others went to the body on the street and examined it by match light.

"This man's been shot," one said. "Right along the top of the skull. Damned ugly furrow, that is. Looks like he might have been run over after that. His neck's mashed awful bad."

"You know who this is, Ben? This here is Alec Lundy, the son of the gunsmith who owns this place. Hey, look there! The front door is partly open."

The gunshot corpse of Arthur Lundy was quickly found inside and policemen summoned.

The woman who had seen the gun-bearing male had already absconded, eager to be safe in her home, but a policeman followed and intercepted and questioned her closely about what she had witnessed.

"Did you recognize the man with the pistol?"

"I don't know his name, and it was dark, but I think I've seen him before. I think he is the son of that Irish seamstress who lives in the rooms up above the old grocery on Chandler Street."

"I've seen that woman. Got young children to raise alone because her husband is dead. Name of Kerrigan, I think. Kate Kerrigan."

He started to make a comment about Kate Kerrigan's remarkable beauty, then bit off the words. Not the right thing to talk about under such circumstances, especially with a woman.

"Yes, sir, officer. Kerrigan. That sounds right. And I do think it was her boy I saw. One of her sons works in Mr. Lundy's gun smithy."

"We may be back around to see you with some more questions, Mrs. Mott. Do you still live over on Danforth Lane?"

"I do, officer. My husband is —"

"Owns the feed store, yes Ma'am. I've traded with Charlie before, myself. Got a few horses on a little farmstead north of. Thank you, Mrs. Mott. We'll find this Kerrigan boy and put all these pieces together. Until we know something different, it looks like we've got a case of a young fellow killing his employers and stealing at least a pistol, and maybe more. We'll know better when we've had time to look through the inventory and cash box."

"Bless you, officer. I'm glad to have you out keeping our streets safe."

"Just my job, Ma'am. That's all."

"Well thank you just the same."

"We'll get that Kerrigan boy and have some answers from him, don't you fret."

CHAPTER EIGHTEEN

Arnold Cheatham was lucky and knew it. An esoteric, intellectual man who felt at home only in the world of academia, he realized how rare a situation he enjoyed.

If not for the fact his late father had been his exact opposite — an earthy, uneducated man who had built up a small fortune through sheer hard labor as a builder of houses for people of means — Arthur Cheatham would have never had the chance to build up the extensive collection of rare books that were his passion, even like his family.

A single man who claimed to be a widower, he had never been forthcoming with many believable details about his long-gone wife or the circumstances of her death, or of their marriage before it.

Not one portrait of the woman hung on the walls of his nicely outfitted house on the edge of Nashville. Many believed his claim of a prior marriage to be a fabrication to help him shun away the inevitable speculation that he might be a good catch for the plainest daughter of some fond mama.

Cheatham had in his employ a young fellow who loved books as much as he did, Quinn Kerrigan, second son of a local Irish widow who managed, somehow, to keep her family afloat with her hard-earned income from seamstress work and occasional dress-tailoring.

Quinn, a bespectacled, somewhat shy boy who looked more like a twelve-year-old than the fourteen-year-old he was, had the same sort of academic bent that Cheatham possessed.

A lover and constant devourer of books, particularly classics of literature and poetry, Quinn had made a point of meeting and getting to know Cheatham when he heard an Irish-born washerwoman who did Cheatham's laundry talk about the huge library that took up more than half of the space in his house.

Quinn felt weak at the knees just in pondering the potential delight of gaining access to such a treasure chest of volumes, and made it his goal to somehow gain it.

It came about more easily than he could have hoped. Lacking any handy pretext to wrangle a meeting with the man, whom most considered an "idler" because he enjoyed the privilege of living, however frugally, off inherited money plus the occasional overpriced sale of oil landscapes that he turned out with ease because they were all essentially the same much-practiced image, Quinn simply gathered his courage, walked up to the door, and knocked.

He'd chanced to do so on a day Cheatham was deeply involved in sorting and categorizing his private library, and growing frustrated with the job. When the young, round-faced Irish lad appeared at his door and all but pleaded for the chance merely to look at Cheatham's collection, the visit led around to an offer of work.

"After you leave your job at the carriage works if you could devote a few hours a week to my library it would be a great help," Cheatham said.

Quinn readily agreed, hardly believing his luck.

"Good, then you will bring order to chaos, and of course I'll pay you for your trouble."

Cheatham said he'd throw in some basic schooling and when Quinn told him of his sisters and brother, he expanded the tutoring offer to include them.

Quinn saw right through Cheatham, or

thought he did.

He knew his mother was considered one of the unmarried beauties in the city. Cheatham probably knew it, too, and was using Quinn and his siblings as an inroad to the Kerrigan family, positioning himself to gain the trust, admiration, and affection of Kate Kerrigan.

Quinn was amused that the man thought he could get away with such a transparent and self-serving ruse.

As time went by and the library gained better and better order and the Kerrigan youngsters became increasingly adept pupils, Quinn had to admit to himself that he was wrong.

Cheatham seemed to like Kate Kerrigan as he got to know her, but his kind of liking was not of the sort Quinn had expected.

There seemed nothing romantic or amorous in his attentions to the Kerrigan family's beautiful young matriarch.

Indeed, he had a demonstrated propensity to bore her to distraction with endless talk of his literary studies, his hope of someday being situated to establish an academy in Nashville, and of his beloved library, which would form the core of that academy's literary collection.

"That is wonderful, Mr. Cheatham," Kate

often told. "A most singular idea and an admirable one."

Then she'd go back to her sewing while Cheatham, seated, as an honored guest, in the Kerrigan family's only overstuffed and comfortable chair, droned on without respite, numbing Kate's mind with his talk of books and authors.

"Do you think Mr. Arthur wants to marry you?" Quinn asked his mother once after Cheatham had spent two long hours trying to teach the basics of Latin to the brother-and-sister twins of the family, Ivy and Niall, age nine in this year of 1867.

"I have my doubts that he will ever wish to marry any woman," Kate replied. "I think the man is already married to his books and his learning."

She had paused before adding, "There are men and women in this world who can love but once in a lifetime. I am such a woman, and I suspect Mr. Cheatham is such a man."

"He never mentions his wife," Quinn said.

"Perhaps his memories are too painful," Kate said.

"All we do is work in books and talk about the same kinds of things he talks about when he is here. He says nothing of his former life."

"A dull life it must be for him, alone in

his house with his dusty books."

"I don't think so, Mother. He seems very content."

"God bless him, then. I cannot see for the soul that's in me how anyone could be happy like that. I mean, do not all of us want family about to call one's own?"

"Not everyone thinks that way, Mother. Priests and nuns, you know."

Kate remembered then that Quinn had at times expressed interest in possibly entering the priesthood. As a woman who hoped someday to have several grandchildren bearing the surname of her beloved late husband, Kate had avoided thinking much about having one of her sons become a celibate man of God.

Surely it would be a fine thing for her son to serve the Almighty, but the priesthood?

It did not fit with Kate Kerrigan's vision for her male children.

"Yes, Quinn," she had said to him. "There are those who are called to turn away from the usual ways of the world and the flesh, but that is a special calling, only for those who are made for it. Perhaps one of them is you, but I must confess both to you and God that I hope it is not. It is a good thing for a man to have a woman and a woman a man, as your father and I had one another.

I hope the same treasure will be give to you someday."

Quinn had looked around and spoke more softly when he replied. "Mother, I told Trace that I might become a priest, and he laughed at me. He said that I'd not be able to give up . . . give up . . . girls and all such things."

Kate smiled. "That is the way God has made us, son. And even though those who put their lives into service of the Church must shun that part of themselves, even it bears no evil in itself. A man and a woman are meant to come together and bring forth life into God's world, as your father and I brought forth you and your brothers and sisters."

"But maybe Mr. Cheatham is different."

"He is a creation of God, as I am, and loved of Christ. But yes, he may be . . . different."

"But he is good, I think."

"He has been quite good to us, saints' truth! The money he pays you to help him with his books, the schooling he has given all of you — and me, too, just from listening while I sit and stitch — he has been a good man to the Kerrigan family, indeed. As dear Mr. Lundy has been good to us in hiring Trace in his gun shop."

■ ■ ■ ■

The day Alec Lundy killed his own father and then met his own death under the wheels of a wagon, Trace Kerrigan did not go home from the gun shop.

As he walked along through alleys and back streets, avoiding as many eyes as possible and hiding the fancy Colt beneath his jacket, his mind examined what had happened and put the pieces together.

It was obvious to him that Alec had shot and killed his own father, using the very Colt now in Trace's possession, then dropped the weapon and somehow died on the street in front of the gun shop.

Trace had not had an opportunity to examine Alec's corpse closely enough to ascertain what had happened. Maybe Arthur had defended himself with his own weapon, and killed Alec even as Alec killed him.

That was the best surmise Trace could make.

It was stunning, and terrible — but the worst part for Trace was that he had been seen exiting the gun shop with the gun in his hand.

He could not hope to avoid suspicion, or

to go uncaught if he went home again. He was boy of the streets enough to know places he could hide himself, but somehow he had to get word to his family. And probably get away from Nashville.

Though he had been unconscious during the final fatal interaction, whatever it had been, no one was left alive who knew that except for Trace himself. Circumstantial appearances were not in his favor.

From the gun shop, Trace made his way in a half-hour tense hike to an old and empty barn standing behind a boarded-up farmhouse just south of town.

The house was empty, too, the widower who had owned it and the farm having died nearly two years earlier. None of his children lived in the region nor had interest in doing so, and the property had been put up for sale, at too high a cost for such rough and unpromising property. The usual process of offer and counteroffer had gotten nowhere, the mercenary heirs being unwilling to settle on a realistic price. None of which mattered at the moment to Trace Kerrigan, who cared only that the place was empty, and far enough from the main part of the city to seldom attract residency by vagrants, drunks, and the like. If he proved lucky, he'd find a good, hidden, dry place in which to hide himself for the night and maybe longer if that should be necessary.

But somehow, somehow, he had to find a way to get news to his mother without going home.

Certainly the local police force would watch the street where the Kerrigans lived, and the area around it. They might even have paid off some of the people of the street to let them know if Trace was seen, and reveal him.

It was a trying situation and a dangerous one.

CHAPTER NINETEEN

The empty farm was as dark and lifeless as usual, which encouraged Trace but did not make him relax. A dark building could yet hide a man and his bottle of rum or his pipe of opiates.

Trace himself, after all, was counting on being able to make himself invisible in the shadows without giving hint of human presence in what looked like an empty piece of property.

So he approached the old farm quietly, the uncurried land around it bladed with moonlight and shadow, and his heart raced.

From somewhere close, probably in a stand of wild oak behind the barn, an owl asked his question of the night and a pair of hunting coyotes, recent immigrants to Tennessee, yipped back and forth.

Beyond the sudden yowl of two cats he interrupted in a moment of feline hostility, all was quiet and nothing moved as he approached the house.

Even so he kept a sharp eye out, glad in that regard for the moonlight even while aware that the same illumination was a danger to him if anyone was in fact in the vicinity.

He reached the base of the stairs leading onto the roofed front porch of the dark and silent house, cussed softly at the pugnacious cats that had startled him, and climbed to the darkest corner of the porch and sat down there, leaning back against the house.

He marveled at the level of tension passing like electricity through his body. Trace had never shunned trouble, sometimes almost looked for it, and even at his young age already had a few pugilism scars that seemed destined to linger for life.

Never before, though, had he faced a situation this dangerous. He almost certainly was already suspected in at least one death.

Maybe I shouldn't have run, he thought. *Makes me look guilty, I reckon . . . but who would believe what little part of the truth I know? And when the deaths happened, I was out cold on the ground.*

The longer he sat, the more he worried about his mother's inevitable concern about his failure to come home.

Every impulse in him told him to go to

her, reassure her, but would it be better for her to see him snatched away by constables on the street than to live with a time of uncertainty?

He did not know the answer, and so remained where he was, listening into the night, until he was nearly certain the house was empty.

He had heard no sound of movement inside, no pricking of the intuition to tell him someone was there.

Trace rose and his eyes scanned the dark landscape within his view, and he moved to a window just to the right of the door missing the timber slats that covered the others.

In moments his arm was inside and the latch turned, and in less time than that the window was raised and he was inside, lowering it again.

He felt more alone inside the house than he had outside, but also more protected with walls around him.

Knowing he could do nothing to alert his mother as to his situation, and that in fact he truly didn't really know what his situation was, he decided to sleep, if he could, and leave the facing of perplexing challenges until morning.

As far as Trace could see in the gloom, no real furniture remained in the house except for a heavily varnished old oak wardrobe, a couple of rickety chairs, and a corncob mattress laid out on the floor in a corner. It smelled like a dirty hay barn, but at least the tick would provide him something softer than a wood floor to sleep on.

He lay on his back right away, there being nothing else for him to do.

Sleep, though, was pushed aside for more than an hour by the worries besetting him, and now, for the first time since it had happened, the loss of Arthur Lundy began to play on Trace's emotions.

The old man had been very good to him and taught him enough of his trade that Trace felt confident that, even if no grander opportunities ever arose for him, he'd be able to make his way as a gunsmith.

There was still much to learn about that craft, but Trace's time with old Lundy had taught him that he had a native talent for gun work, and the ability to enhance it with experience.

It was a good thing to know in a nation that was expanding westward in a way that would invest much reliance in guns. He owed much to old Lundy.

Hard to believe, still, that the animosity between father and son had run so deep.

And strange that both had died on the

same night, in the same place, as though it had been destined. And that Trace Kerrigan, of all people, had been the one situated to fall under suspicion.

He picked up the Colt and held it up so that a ray of moonlight through the window caught it.

It was a beautiful weapon, no question, a shining Excalibur fit for a king, so finely tuned and balanced that Trace had hardly felt the kick of it when he fired it in the back lot.

Odd, Trace pondered, how something as kindly intentioned as the gift of a mere gun had been the spark that ignited the ready tinder of a hate-ruined father and son relationship.

What if the old man had never given it to him? Would he and Alec still be alive?

Before Trace could ponder the answer to that question, a man's voice came quiet and hollow out of the darkness.

"That's a fine looking revolver, Trace."

The words emerged from the far corner, where the shadow of the big wardrobe was thick.

The Colt came up fast and Trace said, "Identify yourself and state your intentions."

"Hell, don't shoot me with that fancy gun.

It's me, Trace. It's Willie Tobin as ever was."

Trace managed to get his lungs working again; they'd shut down the moment he heard the unexpected voice.

He also relaxed his grip on the Colt. He'd grasped it so tightly he could still see the white of his knuckles.

"Willie? What the blazes? I might have killed you, surprising me like that!"

"Aye, indeed, and it was my most fervent hope and prayer you wouldn't. And you haven't."

"Not yet, anyway. Why are you here?"

"If the truth be told I'm hiding, Trace," the street peddler said. "My wife has been unfaithful to me, wedding vows be damned. She's been bumping herself against Tom Grant, the bartender, of all scoundrels, and when I caught them at it, red-handed and bare-bottomed in my own bed, they decided it was time to put an end to old Willie here, and clear the way for their adulteries to go on more free and easy, like. Frank has been hunting me ever since, vowing to end my days."

"Sorry to hear that, Willie," Trace said.

Sorry, but not surprised.

Half the population of Nashville's Irish community had known for months that Martha Tobin had been carrying on with the flashy Tom Grant. Willie was one of the few people in the dark about the situation. It was inevitable he would find out sooner or later.

"Why are you here, Trace? Why aren't you home under the wing of that lovely mother of yours?"

Tobin, a frequent vagrant when Martha threw him out of the house, had edged into touchy territory now.

Many times Trace had heard the man express his admiration for Kate Kerrigan as an object of beauty, though in Tobin's case the more accurate word would be *lust* rather than *beauty.*

Once, out on the street, Trace had chanced to overhear Tobin make an extraordinarily foul and perverse joking remark about Kate's physique, and only the fact Trace was carrying a crate of pistol parts to the gun shop at the time had kept him from going after the man.

Time, and the fact that he otherwise had always gotten on well with Dublin Willie Tobin, had cooled Trace's ire.

"I'm here for the same reason you are, Willie. I'm hiding."

"From who?"

"The law."

"By the saints! What have you done, Trace?"

"That's the rub, Willie, that's the rub. Not a thing. I just had the misfortune to be about when Mr. Lundy and his worthless son decided it was time to kill one another. The sum of the problem for me is, I was seen leaving the gun shop with this pistol in my hand earlier tonight, right after the time they died."

"Then Lundy father and son are dead, then?"

"As of earlier this evening, yes."

"You saw it?"

"Saw their corpses, but not the actual deaths. I had the misfortune to be knocked unconscious by Alec and whenever and however they managed to die, I was not awake to see it."

"Trace, you sure you didn't do for them?"

"No, Willie. I didn't kill them. I swear on my mother's Bible. But as drunk and angry as both of them were before I had my pins knocked from beneath me, I'm not full surprised it ended as it did. There were hard feelings there with those two, Willie. Hard as anvil iron. As best I can figure it, they killed one another."

"Aye. I've overheard arguments a time or two through open windows. But Lord above!

To think of them as dead. I can't get myself to quite believe it."

"It's true. And by noon tomorrow the whole city will know of it. You're well aware of how such things spread. And I'm not fool enough to think I won't be held a suspect. That's why I've taken refuge here."

"And right you are to do it, too. And Dublin Willie gives you his word here and now that no one will learn of our meeting here tonight. Willie's eyes have seen naught, nor his ears heard a peep."

"Thank you, Willie." Then came a realization. "Except, Willie, you can be a great help to me."

"You say the word. I'm a right helpful man. Willie Tobin by name, Willie Tobin by nature I always say."

Trace lost that last comment somewhere along the way.

He said, "My family doesn't know, and I'm loath for them to learn of it from the police, who will tell them, no doubt, that I'm the guilty one."

"Damned police! Hate 'em, I do."

"Most times I have no quarrel with them," Trace said. "It's different now."

"Aye."

"I can't risk trying to go home, Willie. They'll be watching. But somebody has to get the word to my family. The true word, not false police suspicions."

"I'm your pigeon for that job, Trace. I'll carry the good word right to your mother."

The image of Dublin Willie speaking to his mother was distressing.

Kate was fully aware of Willie's obsession with her and the crudity of his interest. She found the man loathsome and had made no secret of it within her family, warning her daughters to avoid the man.

Trace would not create a situation forcing Kate to face Dublin Willie.

"I want you to talk to my brother, Quinn, not to my mother. He will be able to tell her this news in a way that will be easiest for her to bear. You know my brother, I think, at least by sight."

"I do. But I don't mind at all to go to your ma . . ."

"No, Willie. Talk only to Quinn. Tell him I am being forced to hide from a false suspicion, and that it is indeed false. Tell him he and others may be questioned by the police about me. Do not tell him where I am. But tell him that, for now, I am safe and well, and will be with them soon, when I can. Tell him you found me hidden, but that I am not staying where you found me. I must get away from here for my own safety."

"When do I go to young Quinn?"

"As soon as you can. Tell Quinn what I've told you. No one else."

"I shall. And you will later speak well of me to your fine mother for it, eh, right?"

Trace did not bite that hook. "Repeat to me what you are to tell Quinn, Willie."

He did, satisfactorily.

"Do not talk to the police. If they collar and press you, you saw nothing of me tonight."

"Aye, Trace. So it will be. But before I go, there is something you must know. There is someone in town asking after your mother."

"Who?"

"A stranger. A man with but one leg. He says he has something to give Kate Kerrigan."

"Did you talk to him?"

"I did not. But I heard him speaking to Pete Smith the blacksmith, asking where he might find the family of Kate Kerrigan so that he might give her something she is intended to have."

"What does he have for her?"

"Something he said your father gave to him to give her. Something to tell her how to go on without him."

Trace stood silent, puzzling.

"I'll be gone now," Tobin said. "Your family will know you are well soon, I promise."

"Willie, thank you. And remember, only Quinn. You'll find him most evenings at Arnold Cheatham's house buried under a pile of dusty books."

Tobin nodded.

"I know Cheatham. I sold him shoelaces and pins a time or two."

Dublin Willie Tobin climbed through the window and vanished into the night, and Trace was again alone.

CHAPTER TWENTY

Morning came and with it an almost over-whelming impulse to leave the empty old farmhouse and move about normally.

That impulse died fast when Trace looked out the window and spotted a couple of policemen scouting the area.

They had no dog and he breathed a sigh of relief. The keen nose of a bloodhound was the last thing he needed.

But at least the weather was cooperating. Since early that morning it had been raining hard, a steady downpour that fell from a broken sky and hissed like a steam kettle.

The two cops stopped and studied the house, their oilskin capes shedding streams of rainwater.

Trace watched them through a hole in a ragged curtain that lingered from the days the house was occupied. He had no doubt that the city's constabulary was on alert, and all the town talking about the odd and shocking passing of the town's best gun-smith and his son.

Who could have done such a thing, the townsfolk would ask one another. Why, it could only be that Irish boy who was seen coming out of the smithy with a pistol in his hand.

That handsome young Kerrigan boy.

Trace all but held his breath and remained still as the policemen came to the ivy-shrouded front gate and studied the house intently.

Advice his father had given him years before sounded in his mind: "In most of what you face, son, you'll make it through if you don't give in to panic."

He felt some relief when the policemen looked away and one of them said something and nodded his head in the direction of the porch.

The other seemed to agree and Trace stepped back from the window as boots thudded onto the porch.

A moment later he heard the rustle of paper sacks as the lawmen removed lunch-time sandwiches from the pockets of their frocked coats, then their voices as they talked around the food stuffed in their mouths.

Trace recognized both the officers, having

passed time with them on many occasions as they made their rounds in the vicinity of the gun shop.

One of the pair, Harold Simpkins, he didn't much like because he was an incessant chatterer who included needless and annoying interruptions when anyone else was talking.

Trace strained to hear what they might be talking about, as if he couldn't guess, but it was hard to pick up more than scraps of sound. ". . . and no sign of him having gone home, they said. Which shows him as likely guilty."

". . . Probably miles from here by now."

". . . Scrappy fellow, he is, uh-huh, got fine features like his mother, looks to be more a man than his years really make him. Lot different from that baby-faced brother of his. That one's destined to come to a bad end as ever was. He's got the makings, you mark my words."

"Now, you don't know that, Harold Simpkins, no matter how much you fret over it."

"Why else would he go day after day to that Cheatham fellow's place, Jonesy, huh? That man Cheatham is secretive, keeps to himself behind locked doors, and I believe there's many a murder in Nashville that could be laid at his doorstep."

"Murders?" Jonesy said. "There's no proof of that."

"Do you know how many whores were murdered in Nashville this last six months?" Simpkins said.

Jonesy tried to utter some words, but the other cop stomped all over them.

"Five," Simpkins said. "I believe a man in this city is down on whores, and that man is Arnold Cheatham."

"Did you tell the inspector this?" Jonesy said.

"No, I've kept my own counsel. But I'll get him. I'll catch him in the act one foggy night and do for him."

"Well, I won't argue with you. But they say he was married once, but I've always took him for a born gospel shooter with that long Yankee face of his."

"He'll turn that boy to murder, if he ain't already. You mark what I say on that."

"Well, you may be right, Harold, or you may be wrong. Hey, we going to look through the house here in a minute?"

"Reckon so. If Kerrigan's been in there we might find some sign of it. Guarantee you that he ain't in there still, even if he was. Long gone by now, I say. Let me finish this sandwich afore we go in."

It is not the way of law officers to take the

obvious route into a building. They ignored the open window and kicked down the door.

Hearing the splinter of wood, Trace pulled off his boots, quietly rose and walked in his woolen socks over to the wardrobe in the corner.

Though he'd expected it to be weak and rickety, it was, fortunately for his intentions, quite stout, made of heavy thick-cut oak, and put together tightly with screws rather than nails.

Standing beneath a leak-free part of the roof, the wardrobe was not at all afflicted with rot, either wet or dry variety. And the top was broad and flat, and fenced about by the top extensions of the side and front planks.

Trace heard the door on the lower floor creak open and knew the exploration of the house had begun.

Harold Simpkins's voice carried up the staircase, loud enough, Trace noticed, to cover whatever sound he might make doing what he had in mind to do.

"Look's like nobody's lived here in a coon's age," Simpkins said. "Like they all just up and left."

"Here," his partner said, "you don't suppose it was the cholera?"

"Does it linger in the air?" Simpkins said.

"This place has been shut up, you know."

"I don't know if it stays around or not, but let's make this quick," the other cop said. "My belly is starting to hurt."

"For a man that just ate four cheese and pickle sandwiches, that's not surprising," Simpkins said. "But you're right, we'll search the place real quick and leave. I want no part of cholera or spooks either for that matter."

Hiding inside the wardrobe would be obvious and ineffective. They would not expect him to climb atop it. So to the top it would be.

Securing his left foot against the top of the wainscot spanning the wall, Trace heaved himself up, laid his boots quietly on the top of the wardrobe, and then scrambled up, trying to make no sound.

He was pleased to hear the policemen chatter on about ha'ants and such, and hoped the wooden cornice at the top of the high armoire would suffice to hide him if he lay as flat as he could.

The rectangular wardrobe top, though expansive, would not quite allow him to stretch out fully unless he hung his feet over the side that faced into the corner of the room.

He was assessing whether it was safer to

risk doing that or to lie on his side and hope none of him showed over the top front of the boxy piece of furniture, when he heard their footsteps on the stairs.

"Trace Kerrigan? You in here, boy?" The voice was of Harold Simpkins.

Trace, with no further time for self debate, opted to hang his socked feet over the hidden side of the wardrobe top. He lay on his belly and made himself as flat as possible, grateful for his thin build.

"Look there, Jonesy — there's a tick mattress over in the corner," Simpkins said.

"Yeah. Can you tell if anybody's been sleeping on it?"

Trace listened to the policeman cross the room. "Can't really tell. No blankets or nothing on it."

Harold opened the wardrobe door and looked inside. "Ain't in here."

Trace bit his lips and tensed.

Don't think about the top, Harold. Nobody's on the top of this thing, no sir. Not a soul.

"Don't know where he is, but he ain't here, Jake," Simpkins said.

"Never expected him to be," Jonesy said. "I got a nose for these things. Knowed all along he wouldn't be. He ain't going to linger hereabouts, not with the trouble he's facing."

Then they were gone and all that remained was the hammer of the rain and the distant roar of thunderclouds tearing their guts out on the craggy peaks of the Appalachians.

Trace remained where he was for a while, in case the police were baiting him, hoping to lure him out from wherever he was hiding.

After ten minutes he climbed down from the armoire, pulled his boots on, and left by the door in the old pantry room at the rear of the house.

After some cautious prowling around, he satisfied himself that the policemen were gone.

Trace's heart slowed to normal and then he began to think about food. That and getting as far away from Nashville as fast as he could.

He had to trust that Willie would do as he said and get the message to Quinn. He would not be free to go home himself for God only knew how long.

Suddenly he was no longer the tough young hellion he liked to see himself as, but a boy very much in need of seeing and receiving advice from his mother.

Thoughts of Kate Kerrigan reminded him of what Willie had said about a stranger being in town, asking after her.

That was really odd.

Would Willie have concocted the mysterious story in hope of bringing about a chance to make face-to-face contact with Kate?

Probably so.

A stranger bearing something from his father, dead now for five years, to be given to his mother? It made little sense.

Trace tucked his Colt under his belt in a way to let his coat hide it, then entered some woods and began a southward hike that at length brought him into a broad, rolling field with a single hardwood tree in the middle.

Despite the rain, as Trace walked closer to the tree he startled a flock of crows roosting in the branches. The birds fluttered into the air like pieces of charred paper and caw-cussed Trace for an interloper.

Where he was going or what he would do the young man did not know.

What mustn't happen was to let himself stumble into the welcoming arms of the law.

Though he'd done nothing, even he had to admit that the circumstances made him look as guilty as hell.

He trudged on, knowing he needed to find something to eat if he was to maintain his strength for whatever lay before him.

■ ■ ■ ■

Two hundred yards across the field, he stopped and looked back around the edge of the woods and toward the outskirts of his town.

Within the bounds of Nashville his mother was probably at work, hands flying with needle and thread, a new garment being made, or repaired, or decorated. All Kate Kerrigan's work was done well, which made Trace proud.

As the eldest child, he knew better than the others the value of his mother's character, skill, and dedication.

She'd persuaded him, merely by the way she had lived her life and persevered through so much pain, loss, and hardship, that there was nothing she could not do if she dedicated herself to it.

And the same, he figured, held true for him, too, as her son.

He missed his father, he and Quinn having been old enough to remember him.

He recalled some of what Joe Kerrigan had taught him, and tried hard to follow it.

Even so, it was his mother from whom the best direction and example had come.

He remembered a famous quote from the

late Lincoln — a man many of Nashville's predominately pro-Confederate Irish folk despised, but whom Trace couldn't help but admire on some levels — to the effect that most of the worthy things he had learned in life, he owed to his mother.

Trace understood that fully. It was that way with him, too.

He was not prone to cry, was Trace. It was unmanly. Quinn shed tears over a wounded butterfly, to his everlasting shame, but it was not a Kerrigan thing to put one's emotions on display like that.

But Trace was alone now, accompanied only by his fears and in possession only of the clothes on his back, the boots on his feet, and the fine customized Colt revolver thrust under his belt. And for that he had only enough ammunition pocketed to reload it a few times.

He stared at the low, rough outline of the city where he'd been born, and wished he were free to go back to it and to his secure home again.

He smiled to himself.

Unmanly or not, he missed the luxury of tears.

Chapter Twenty-One

Shannon Kerrigan's health seemed to be improving. Her coughing had grown less frequent and her fever was gone.

Kate's earlier anger at providence was tempered now by seeing that her prayers for her daughter seemed at last to be receiving positive answers.

Shannon was growing well enough that she soon might be up and doing the things that five-year-olds do.

"Mother, I'm thirsty," Shannon said.

Not in her bed now, as she had been for what seemed an eternity of days, Shannon was sitting up and holding a doll her older sister, nine-year-old Ivy, had made for her from scraps given to her by her mother.

The doll wore a plain blue dress Kate had sewn together, also from scraps, and Shannon had named the doll Katie.

"She's named after her grandmother, you see," she said to Kate. "After you."

"I am honored, I think," Kate told the child, and gave her a smile.

Smiles were hard to generate at the moment, despite Shannon's improvement. The situation of Trace was difficult beyond endurance.

Kate was quite sure her son would never have been involved in the deaths of the Lundy father and son, yet she saw realized how bad the matter had to look to others, including the police.

Her greatest fear was not that Trace would be found to be involved in the fatalities, but that he would be found dead himself.

He'd been seen leaving the gun shop with his revolver in hand. Then he'd not been seen since. Had he been wounded by whoever really did the shootings? Might he have gone off and died in some spot where he could not readily be found?

Kate spoke to the police, who assured her that they believed her son was still alive.

"And well?" she said.

"That we cannot say, Ma'am."

The authorities had no clue where Trace was and when Kate suggested she go look for him herself, they dismissed the idea.

Inspector Chariton, a small, scholarly looking man with intelligent brown eyes, said, "Mrs. Kerrigan, we're talking about a crime that involves guns and gunmen here, and both kill people. Search on your own and you launch yourself into dangerous waters and I cannot be responsible for your safety."

"I'm willing to take the chance," Kate said.

"And where would you look? North, east, south, or west? Such a search would take a regiment of horses a week and maybe more. How could you succeed when so far the police have failed, and you are still not much more than a slip of a girl yourself?"

Kate was defiant.

"I'll do whatever it takes to save my son," she said.

Chariton shook his head.

"Mrs. Kerrigan, if I must, I'll place a police guard on your house to prevent you from venturing forth. Now, do not provoke me into such an action."

That frightened Kate.

Suppose Trace tried to come home, perhaps wounded, and saw police at the door?

He might run and keep on running and she'd never see him again.

"Very well, Inspector, I'll do as you say," she said. A bitter pill.

"We'll keep you informed, Mrs. Kerrigan."

"My son didn't kill those men."

"That will be for a court to decide."

"Then bring him in alive, Inspector."

"That will be for Trace to decide," Chariton said.

Almost as worried about Trace as Kate was his brother Quinn.

Despite the significant differences in physique, interest, and temperament between the brothers, Quinn even so idolized his elder brother and secretly envied his good looks and attractiveness to girls. Quinn could only dream of having girls look at him the way they looked at Trace.

He'd decided it would probably never happen, which was one reason he had toyed at times with the idea of becoming a priest.

If he was destined to live with little chance of feminine attentions and affections, why not face reality and enter a world in which there was no expectation of a man cutting a dash, or whatever it was men did to attract pretty girls?

The older Quinn grew, though, the more difficult it was to seriously consider a life devoid of the love of the opposite sex.

If it was as wonderful a thing as Quinn had heard men say, he didn't want to miss out on it, even for such a great cause as serving the Church.

As he worked cataloging hundreds of volumes in Mr. Cheatham's private library, Quinn pondered the question of why it was the man seemed to have little interest in women.

He was not a priest, under no obligation to live without a mate, yet he never spoke of women he had known and loved, or commented to Quinn, as so many men did, about the beauty of Kate Kerrigan.

Quinn had heard from his mother that there were some men who could only care for one woman in a lifetime, and though rare, Arnold Cheatham was one of them. Ma considered it a virtue.

It made Quinn uncomfortable to think about it, living a life without pretty girls around, especially since Mr. Cheatham seemed to love only his books.

Quinn put his strange employer out of his mind, throwing himself into the labor of shelving books. And worrying about Trace.

Where was he? Was he safe and well? Had he actually been involved in the violence that left the Lundy men dead? No, that was impossible.

There was a sharp rapping on the front door and Cheatham called from elsewhere in the house, asking Quinn to answer it.

Quinn climbed down from the library ladder he'd been standing on and went to the door.

Willie Tobin, whom Quinn recalled was a vagabond tinker with wife troubles, stood on the step.

"Hello, Mr. Tobin," he said.

"Hello, Quinn. How fare you?"

"Well enough. Have you come to see Mr. Cheatham?"

"Truth is, I came to see you."

"Me? I have no need for needles and pins today, or money to buy them."

"No sales today, Quinn. Is there a place where I could talk to you privately, like?"

Quinn was instantly ill at ease.

Willie Tobin looked like he'd missed a night's sleep and his last four meals.

But he was certainly no policeman, constable, or deputy, in fact had often been on the wrong side in his relationship with that breed.

So surely whatever he had come to Quinn about was not part of some attempt to ferret out Trace from hiding.

Even so, Kate had warned her children to avoid any casual discussions regarding their oldest brother, because one never knew . . .

Quinn stepped outside and quietly closed the door.

"What can I do for you, Mr. Tobin?"

185

Willie Tobin looked around as though expecting detectives to leap out of the shrubbery. He leaned closer and spoke in a near whisper to Quinn.

"Your brother sent me," he said.

Quinn was instantly suspicious.

Willie Tobin had never been a friend or confidant of any of the Kerrigans, and seemed an unlikely candidate to be playing messenger for Trace.

Quinn looked around, suspecting some sort of police trap.

"You've seen Trace?"

"I have. I had cause to seek a hiding place for myself, and found Trace already settled there. He sent me to give you word to take back to your ma that he is safe and well and will be back with his kin as soon as it is safe to do so. He said he is under false suspicion for something he did not do."

"Yes, he is. But he is well, you say?"

"Indeed, he is."

"I am relieved. Where is he?"

"An empty house. It would be to no avail in trying to find him there now. He will be gone. Would you wish me to go tell your mother, to spare you the need?"

"No. She will be glad to hear Trace is alive and knows to keep himself out of view."

"I'd be glad to tell her, young sir."

"No, I'll do it. But thank you for telling me."

"You were outside for a time?" Cheatham asked Quinn later.

"Yes, I was. A man came to see me and give me some news. He has seen my brother and says he is safe."

"You mustn't spread that information far, my friend. This town is ablaze with talk about the young gunman who is said to have killed those two men."

"I know. But Trace didn't do it. He claims innocence and I believe him."

"Truth sometimes does not matter, Quinn. There are those who have decided what they think your brother is, and nothing will persuade them differently, truth be damned. It is the nature of most human beings to do that. I know it all too well in the experience of my own life."

"Please, sir, don't tell anyone what I have just shared with you. It might make the police feel more sure that Trace is close by, and make them look harder for him."

"No one will hear a word from me, Quinn."

Cheatham paused, looking closely at his young hireling, and rubbed his chin thoughtfully.

"Come with me a moment, Quinn. There is something I want you to see. Something related to what I was saying about the propensity of human beings to prejudge others and then cling to that prejudice no matter how wrongheaded it may be."

The room was small, roughly the size of a humble pantry, and lined with book-laden shelves like much of Arthur Cheatham's dwelling. Quinn had not seen this particular room before, the door usually being closed.

Cheatham went to a particular shelf and removed a volume. He opened it, then motioned Quinn closer.

It was a scrapbook of images, both sketches and photographs, showing the face of a dark-haired young woman, quite pretty. Cheatham sighed as he looked at it.

"Who is she, sir?"

Cheatham looked down at Quinn and smiled. "She was my wife, Quinn. I was once a married man. Are you surprised?"

"I . . . I am, sir."

"Most people are, which is one of the reasons I don't reveal that particular fact to many. I am distressed by their surprise, and the obvious misconceptions they carry regarding me. It causes me to wonder what all might have been said about me out in the town."

"People can be . . . harsh, sir. Unkind."

"I know. Believe me, I know. Harsh, and wrong-thinking."

"What was her name?"

"This is my beloved lost Phoebe. Killed two years into our marriage in a most bizarre accident. A train jumped its track and crashed over the edge of an overpass. Phoebe was in a carriage on the road below, traveling with her sister to a child's baptism. The locomotive crushed the carriage like an egg beneath a big man's boot. I doubt either of them had the slightest awareness of what was happening, it being so swift and . . . destructive."

"Mercy, sir, I'm very sorry."

"Mercy, you say. Oddly enough, the only mercy I could see in Phoebe's loss was the speed of it. There was no time for suffering, or asking unanswerable questions. She was alive, and a moment later, gone."

"You had no children?"

"None. Had she lived, perhaps later, though that chance is now gone."

"How long ago did you lose her?"

"Fifteen years. Long and lonely years they have been. At one time I kept some of these images of her hanging in a small hallway, when I lived in Atlanta. It became too painful to see them so readily, though. Eventually I put them away in this volume, so I could see her face whenever I felt the need of it, but not be subjected to the pain of seeing it at other times."

"Did you ever think of remarrying?"

The question caused Cheatham to grow silent and stare up a few moments into a cobwebbed upper corner of the little room. He spoke at last.

"Quinn, men are not all the same. Not in their appearances, their sizes, races, interests, passions. Or degrees of the latter. Even when I was married to my Phoebe, who was the center of my life and the very beat of my heart, I was not a man of strong passions, if you understand me. But I was not, and never have felt the slightest inclination to be, the kind of man many have avowed that I am."

Cheatham smiled.

"I have no inclination to be a preacher, a priest or whatever else they say, and I am certainly not a murderer. What happened to me was that whatever degree of intimate passions I possessed with Phoebe, well, those passions died with her. When she was gone I never felt drawn, at any level, to another woman. The drive was simply gone. Like Phoebe. And I have lived without feeling its tugs and urgings from that time forward."

"Oh." Quinn had no idea what to say. Then, "But why do they accuse you of being a murderer?"

"Because I'm a man who lives alone and does not much care for the company of others. That makes me different and people who are different are always suspect."

"I wish you could find another Phoebe," Quinn said.

"Well, it's a blessing, in its way. It removes one of the struggles most have to live with. I can immerse myself more deeply in other things I care about — art, literature, history, and anything and all things to do with the world of books. If Phoebe could return to me, perhaps some other things I have lost might return as well. Without her — well, I simply don't care. That is the truth of this sad man who stands before you, my boy."

The conversation was growing awkward and Quinn sought a way to redirect it.

"Did you do those sketches of her face, sir?"

"I did. One of my old hobbies, now seldom pursued. I have nothing left worth sketching, you see."

"She was lovely," Quinn said.

"She defined loveliness, lad. And love

itself. Ah, me!"

"I am sorry you lost her. But at least you had her for a time."

"That, Quinn, is my only consolation. Better to have loved and lost, and all that. It's really true, you know. But the pain, the pain!"

"I understand, sir."

"Quinn, if you would, please go back to what you were doing before. I want to visit with my lost love a few minutes more, and then I'll join you."

"Yes, sir."

Quinn walked home pondering the unusual truths that had come his way that day.

Lost in thought, he didn't notice a man who abruptly blocked his way.

The man had come out of a doorway near the Kerrigan home and Quinn ran into him and almost lost his balance.

"Need to watch where you're going," patrolman Harold Simpkins said as he gripped Quinn by the shoulders and looked down into his startled face. "You ought not run over folks like that."

"I'm sorry, sir. You stepped out in front of me, that's all."

Simpkins laughed. "You're right, boy. I made it happen. And there's other things I can make happen, too."

Quinn just stared, puzzled and alarmed.

Simpkins was a tall, thin, lank man with black eyes and hair and a narrow, pointed chin like Punch from the puppet show. He was a man without conscience and possessed a quick, agile brain.

"Come here, boy," the policeman said, and all but dragged Quinn into the alley beside them. He manhandled Quinn around to face him, and then gripped his shoulders, hard.

"One of the things I can make happen is I can go visit that pretty mama of yours and let her know the kind of things her boy has been doing for that monster you work for."

Quinn found his voice. "Sir, Mr. Cheatham is not a monster of any kind. I help him catalog his books, that's all I do. He's got hundreds of them, and he's trying to get them in good order so he can find the ones he needs when he needs them."

"Did you ever hear him mention Roxy Sinclair?" Simpkins said.

"No, I did not."

"She was Cheatham's last victim, murdered in an alley, her throat cut from ear to ear."

Quinn considered making a dash for it, but he dared not.

"What do you want from me, sir?" Quinn asked, voice quaking.

"I want proof that Cheatham is down on whores, but that can wait," Simpkins said. His breath smelled like raw onions.

"But first I want your brother. I want to find him, get my hands on the murdering scum. I want you to tell me where he is . . . and don't you try to claim you don't know! I guarantee you know!"

"I don't . . . I swear."

"Well, it's your ma who'll be doing the swearing when she hears her little angel boy has been making himself an accomplice to a man who rips whores for fun."

"I am not, sir. I swear before Jesus and the angels that I'm not."

"Get used to saying that, because I can work things out to give you ample chance to say it a lot, to a lot of folk, including a judge."

"Don't do that, sir, please!"

"Why sure, it's easy to shut my mouth. All you got to do is tell me where I can find that murdering brother of yours."

"I haven't seen him, sir, haven't talked to him nor got any word. All I know is he didn't murder anybody."

"You know that for a fact, do you? Were you there when the Lundys were killed?

Speak up, boy."

"No, no sir. But —"

"But what? Go on — out with it!"

Quinn, terrifically frightened now, found himself speaking when he didn't really want to. "I know somebody who *did* see him."

"Was it your ma, you fat little turd? I'd welcome the chance to have a good conversation with that pretty mama you have."

"No."

"Somebody else in your family?"

"No, sir. It was Dublin Willie."

"That worthless rummy? Hell, he probably dreamed he saw him and thought it was real!"

"He said he found him hiding someplace, but he didn't say where. He said Trace wouldn't be there anymore, anyway."

"Running off, I guess. I figured he'd run off."

"He said that Trace told him to tell me that he was fine, and that he hadn't done anything bad no matter what folks were saying."

"I never seen a lawbreaker yet who didn't deny his crimes. Nor have I ever seen an innocent man run from the place a crime has been done. A guilty one, though, he'll run as fleet as a buck deer."

Quinn felt like a betrayer for the information he had given this unpleasant officer, even though there had been no particularly significant information in it. He fought to hold back tears, knowing the policeman would doubtlessly find it amusing if Quinn cried.

"I'm going to have me a little talk with Dublin Willie and see if he really does know anything worth knowing. And if I learn that he told you more than you're saying he did, you little dog-pile, I'm going to go visit your ma and tell her what kind of nasty things her little boy has been up to. You hear me, boy?"

"Yes, sir."

Simpkins shoved Quinn away from him with contempt, then turned and walked back out toward the street. At the end of the alley he turned back to Quinn.

"You mind what I told you, boy. If I want to, and I really want to, I can make your life a living hell and your ma's, too."

"I haven't done anything, sir, and neither has my brother," Quinn said.

Simpkins laughed, and turned to rejoin the street traffic.

He walked right into an Irish blackthorn stick swung by Kate Kerrigan.

The heavy shillelagh crashed into the man's face, broke the bridge of his nose and split the thin skin above his eyes.

His face bloody, eyes already closing, Simpkins hit the ground hard, twitched for a few moments and then he did not move.

Kate didn't wait to see the cop fall.

She grabbed Quinn by the wrist and ran.

"Hurry, son," she said. "I've left oatmeal simmering in the pot."

Harold Simpkins would later say, from his hospital bed, that he didn't know what hit him, but suspected that members of an Irish street gang were involved.

Chapter Twenty-Two

Kate Kerrigan lived in one of the more decrepit sections of the city where, during the war, her house and the streets around it had been surrounded by a virtual tent city.

The tents were inhabited by freed slaves and other wartime refugees and later a small church had been built by the Federal authorities to serve the spiritual needs of a black Baptist congregation.

The church had burned a year after it was constructed, leaving only an arched stone entryway in the midst of a lot that since then had become covered with brush, poison ivy, and sapling trees.

Ignored now by most, the ruin had become a refuge of sorts for Kate Kerrigan, who fancied that the arch had the look of an abandoned monastery cloister.

It was a quiet place where she went when it was essential to clear her mind and be around no one else at all. With cramped living quarters and a family of children, privacy was rare.

Kate considered her secret place, only a stone's throw from her house, vital to maintaining a healthy state of mind.

Here she counseled herself, talked to her dead husband and parents in the certainty they could hear her.

Sometimes she chided God for allowing life to be so hard at times, but those occasions were few.

To Kate's knowledge, no one in her family or circle of acquaintances knew this was her spot. She'd never encountered another person while secreted away in the fire-blackened ruin among the sheltering brush and trees.

That evening, as the older children looked after Shannon, she took a few moments to pray for the speedy recovery of patrolman Simpkins.

Poor man, a blackthorn stick could do terrible things when swung in anger, and the talk of her neighbors was that the injured officer might be in the hospital for at least a week.

"A gang set about him," the neighbors said. "And left him all broken and bloody on the cold ground."

"Serves him right for frightening my

child," Kate wanted to tell them. But she didn't, and settled for, "Well, that's a shame, isn't it?"

She also prayed briefly for Quinn, who had come home from his work at the Cheatham house in a distracted, upset state of mind, but had declined to explain why.

She worried sometimes about him spending so much time with Cheatham, who seemed to her, and many others, a very strange, withdrawn man.

During all the times she'd left the house to visit the old church, Kate had never seen another soul. It was said that the ruin was haunted and that kept people away.

But that evening she had two.

The first was a ghost from a time gone and a noble cause lost.

The moon had begun its rise and the rain clouds had gone when she heard the step of feet coming toward her through the gloom.

Kate stood under the arch, and her eyes searched the crowding darkness.

"Who's there?" she called.

She bit her lip. Probably yet another policeman, be damned to them.

"Mrs. Kerrigan?"

A man's voice, low and unhurried.

"Who is it?" Kate said.

"If you're Kate Kerrigan, you know who I am."

The darkness parted, and a figure wearing an old gray Confederate coat limped toward her.

Kate felt a stab of excitement, not unmixed with apprehension.

"Dear God and his Blessed Mother, Joe is it you?"

"I'm no ghost, Mrs. Kerrigan," the man said. "Am I not Mike Feeny, minus a leg and a cause?"

Feeny stepped into a blade of moonlight.

"Mike, I see it is you," Kate said.

"I'm not Joseph, more's the pity. But I bring his last words to you."

Kate ran to the old soldier's side.

"Mike, I see that you are sore hurt. Did—"

"Joe passed from day into night without pain," Feeny said.

He reached inside his ragged coat.

"This is for you, Mrs. Kerrigan. I've carried it this last five years and hoped one day I would find you. Then, by the grace of God, I saw you leave your house and followed you here. This is the end of the second month I've spent in Nashville searching for you."

Kate took the envelope and Feeny said,

"The blood is mine."

"Mike, there is so much I want to ask you," Kate said. "Will you come home with me and have a cup of tea?"

Feeny shook his head.

"No, I must be on my way."

His eyes softened and a faint smile touched his lips.

"Joe's letter will say all that needs to be said. And there are some things that need to remain unsaid."

Feeny turned away.

"God bless you, Kate," he said.

Then, despite Kate's pleas, he vanished into the darkness.

The envelope, stained with blood, was still sealed after all the years that had passed.

Kate hesitated to open it. She might misread Joe's words in the faded light or drop the letter and not be able to find it again.

But the truth was she feared to read it, lest she break down and return home with a tear-stained face and alarm the children.

Kate shoved the envelope into the pocket of her dress for later, when the hour was late and everyone was asleep.

Now it was time to make for home.

Then the sound of feet rustling through brush.

Had Mike Feeny returned?"

"Don't be frightened, Ma. It's just me."

The voice was unmistakably Trace's, and his tall, slender figure was coming toward her, like a gray ghost in the moonlight.

Kate heard her son's voice again, tinted with a smile.

"Yes, I'm really here."

She gasped and then he was there.

Trace still wore the same clothes he'd worn the day he'd gone off to work at the gun shop, and everything had gone bad.

Perhaps he was a little more ragged, stained and dirty, and his sparse teen-years whiskers a little longer on his jaws.

But it was Trace. This was no dream. It was him.

Kate smiled and went to him, hugging him close and Trace doing the same to her.

She kissed her son's cheek, kissed him again, and tasted the salt of her tears.

"Trace, where did you come from?"

"I've not gone far, only a few miles out of town. I've slept in the woods, in sheds, barns. God forgive me, I even ate an apple pie that was cooling in some farm wife's window. I've done well enough for myself, staying hidden. I've seen policemen looking for me, but they never saw me. I'm good at hiding, Mother. I've proven it, I think."

"How did you get here without being seen?" She looked around. "Did anybody see you?"

"No, Ma. This is a fairly easy place to reach without being seen. The trees and undergrowth stretch all the way out of town, so I figured I could sneak through that way, keeping an eye out so I could hide if I needed to."

"How did you know I would be here?"

"I didn't. But I've known about this spot of yours for a long time now. I followed you out here a couple of times when I was twelve or thirteen, then slipped on back home without you seeing. I never stayed because I could tell this was a private place for you, and I didn't want to bother you."

"Oh, Trace, my son — are you hurt, sick, anything at all?"

"No, neither sick nor hurt. And no matter what you may hear or the police may question people about, I'm innocent, too. See this bruise on my temple? It's starting to fade a little now, but Alec Lundy gave that to me out behind the store. Hit me with a pistol because he was mad that his father had given me a special gun he'd wanted for himself."

Alarmed, Kate raised her hand and investigated Trace's bruised temple in the thickening dusk light.

"It's fine, Ma. And I'm fine. But I was out cold when Alec and Mr. Lundy died. So I don't know for sure how it happened. There was bad blood between them and I think they must have somehow shot each other but I can't quite put it together in my mind."

Kate said, "There's been much gossip, Trace. A doctor said Alec's neck had been broken by a wagon wheel, and he might have died from that. But he'd been shot, too, a head wound."

"I was knocked out," Trace said. "I didn't see or hear much."

"They say you fled, and you had a revolver with you."

"I did. It's the one I carry now, the fine Colt I showed you at the house."

"Is it a cursed thing, now?" Kate said.

"Steel can't be cursed, Ma, it has no soul. If curses there were, perhaps they were on Arthur Lundy who thought higher of me than of his own son. And on Alec who was a dark, envious and violent man."

"Maybe he needed killing," Kate said. "Some men do."

"Well, right or wrong, Lundy gave me the

pistol, and Alec came in drunk and learned of it, and that's when the trouble started."

Trace outlined a brief version of what happened, as best he knew it.

"You're innocent, then, no question about it," Kate said. "Is that not so, Trace?"

"I hope you never believed anything other than that, Ma."

"I did not," she said, smiling and taking his hand. "I know my children."

"I have to stay hidden. For the same reason I had to run away from the gunsmith shop. Because nobody is going to believe the truth."

Kate thought in silence a moment, then nodded.

"I wish that was not true, but true it is," she said. "We will keep you hidden away, Trace, until we can leave here and put this behind us."

"We might have to travel a long way to do that, Mother. This is suspicion of murder we're talking about. The law won't let this drop until they have the Lundys' killer behind bars. It's a serious matter."

"It is. And travel a long way we shall, until it has no hope of catching up to us."

Mother and son talked quietly until the overgrown, ragged little lot was dark, keeping an eye and ear out all the while in case anyone should come near and find them.

Trace declared then it was time for him to slip back out of town again and find another hiding place in which to pass one more fugitive night, but Kate would have none of it.

"It is dark, and I have traveled between home and this place enough times to know there is a way to go that is very hidden. We will get you home, and inside, and no one but folk named Kerrigan will know it. Tonight you will sleep in your own bed, son. You must be gone from it and away even before the sun comes up, but tonight you will stay at your home. This situation I must explain to the entire lot of us, and you should be there to hear it, too."

"Ma, I can't even dare go in the door. I would be seen by somebody, and the police would —"

"You do not need a door, son. Not with a strong rose trellis rising along the back of the house."

They made their way home again without difficulty and without detection.

Kate left Trace loitering in the shadows at the base of the rose trellis, and quietly went in and told the children that something was about to happen that might make them want to shout, but shouting must not be done.

Quiet was essential because there were eyes that watched them and ears that listened.

"I am going to say something now, and I want not so much as a gasp of surprise from any of you. We cannot risk an outburst that might rouse suspicions of those who might hear."

"What is it, Mother?" asked Niall, the youngest boy.

Kate leaned forward and touched her finger to her lips. "Trace is here," she whispered.

Ivy almost squealed, but squelched it.

Kate smiled at her children and thanked them for holding silent. Smiles beamed all around.

"We must continue to be quiet as Trace comes in," she said. "No one of us would want to be responsible for our brother being dragged away by the coppers because we made noise, now, would we?"

Heads shook with great vigor.

"Very good, then. Now . . . quietly."

They went to a rear window in the bedroom shared by the boys, and at Kate's behest, Quinn opened it gently.

He stepped back as the trellis that reached

up beside the window began to shake. Moments later, Trace was sticking a leg through the open window, followed by the rest of him.

They hustled him to a place where no windows allowed a view in from the exterior, and Trace received more hugs and whispered welcomes than a hero of soldier returning from war.

Kate could not hold back her tears, and soon they flowed from every eye in the dwelling.

Trace was alive and safe, and for the moment, anyway, he was home.

CHAPTER TWENTY-THREE

Kate Kerrigan called for no interruptions, then took time to read the letter from her husband by dim firelight.

By the time she finished there were tears in her eyes but hope in her heart.

Five years had dulled the pain of Joe's death, but hurt there still was and it remained an open wound that would never heal.

As it was, the Kerrigan family's celebration was of necessity muted and did not last long. Even excessive movement of human forms to and fro past the windows might be seen as an indication of excitement within the house, and draw a patrolman's loud knock to the door.

But every eye had been on Kate as she read the letter, and even little Shannon, her eyes as round as coins, had said nothing until she saw her ma wipe away the last of her tears and smile.

"What is it, Ma?" Shannon said, upset because her mother was upset.

"I'll tell you in a moment," Kate said. "Come closer, children, you, too, Trace, and listen to what I have to say."

She looked around the circle of attentive faces, the letter held on her lap.

"God works in mysterious ways," she said. "And this night that miracle came in the form of an old, one-legged soldier by the name of Mike Feeny who was with your father when he died."

Trace was confused.

"This evening? You mean he came here?"

"No, to the ruined church," Kate said. She smiled. "Two miracles on the same night and in the same place, huh, Trace?"

"Tell us of the first, Ma," Trace said. "The second is of less importance."

"They are both equally important," Kate said.

Then, her beautiful face illuminated by the fire, she said, "Our lives are about to change and for the better. All of you children were born and raised in this city and have known no other place as your home. But soon to we are going to leave Tennessee and have a great adventure."

"Why, Mother?" asked Ivy, frowning. The nine-year-old said, "I have friends in Nashville and don't want to move away and leave them."

"I said we were leaving on a great adventure," Kate said. "But in the course of that enterprise we will all have to make sacrifices."

"I don't want to leave my friends," the girl said, her little face stubborn.

"Ivy, Trace's life is in terrible danger and if he's caught a hangman's rope awaits him," Kate said. "He was seen running out of the gunsmith where he worked with a pistol in his hand. There were two men found dead there, and the police suspect Trace of the killing."

"You didn't do it, did you, Trace?" asked Niall.

"Of course not!" Trace whispered back, nervous even about speaking at a normal volume. "What a stupid thing to ask me."

Niall, looking chagrined, turned away and eyed his mother.

"Trace," Kate gently chided. "He was just trying to be sure. Children see everything in black and white. There are no shades of gray between."

"I know. I know. I'm just tired of being suspected of something I didn't do, and having to hide like a rat in a wall."

"Well then why did you run, Trace?" asked Quinn.

Trace glared at his younger brother.

"I was scared, real scared. You would have run, too."

"No, I wouldn't. I would have shot it out with the police, stolen a horse and rode away into the woods," Quinn said.

"That's enough, boys," Kate said. "We all know Trace didn't do anything wrong."

"So then why are we leaving and where are we going, Mama?" Ivy asked.

Kate breathed slowly and tried to relax.

A moment had come she had never anticipated and now wasn't fully ready to handle.

"Children, your father wrote this letter" — she held it up where all could see — "to me before his final battle. He carried it into the fight, and it was found on him after he died and Mike Feeny brought it to me tonight.

"Much of the content expresses your pa's love for his family, of his wish he could leave war behind and be with us, and his hopes for a bright future for the Kerrigan family."

Kate brushed away a random curl that had fallen over her forehead.

"But he gave us, well, me, a word of advice should he not come home from the war. It is advice that I think will change our lives greatly, but cannot be done without the firmest dedication and hard work from all of us."

"Mother, please —" Trace said.

"I'm getting to the point, Trace, be patient. With such a pressing need to leave this city upon us, I've decided to heed your father's advice."

After a moment's pause as she waited for the excitement to build, Kate said, "We will leave Tennessee by way of Kansas, then travel to Texas, there to enter the cattle business, which your father believed is destined to bring great success to many people."

Quinn looked stunned, Niall confused, and Ivy put her hands to her face and cried. Frail little Shannon clapped lightly and looked thrilled, while it was all Trace could do to keep in his seat.

Unspoken to many, a move west had been Trace's dream since he was eight years old, a dream old Arthur Lundy had reignited before his death.

Kate surmised that Joe had probably done some further talking in the meantime with Texan soldiers who knew the facts of the cattle trade.

Clearly he'd been persuaded that it was a business the Kerrigans could truly be part of.

And now that Joe was gone, she saw it as falling to her to make his vision a reality.

Trace looked at his mother's face, smiled and nodded. She nodded back, a little more solemn than he, but the hint of a smile was there.

"Well, then it's settled," Kate said. "Texas or Bust. Isn't that what the pioneers used to say?"

"That's what they said, Ma," Quinn said. "I read it in a book."

"And now you're going to live it," Kate said. "All of us."

CHAPTER TWENTY-FOUR

Due to the hunt for Trace, Kate felt that leaving Nashville was more like a desperate escape.

Over the next days, the family had no choice but to abandon many of their possessions, because for them to be seen emptying their living space would have caused an entirely accurate perception that they were running from the legal difficulties facing Trace, who now was officially wanted by the authorities "on suspicion of murder or manslaughter."

"It's for the best," Kate told her children around the breakfast table two days after Trace's visit home. He'd remained only that one night, shinning back down the trellis before dawn and going back into hiding.

Using the little amount of money Kate gave him, her son was going it alone. His plan was to escape Nashville by dark, and then hopefully buy a cheap horse and saddle that could carry him to Kansas.

Kate had not heard from Trace since and she worried constantly about him. This much she knew, the police had not found him yet or they would have told her.

No news was good news, the saying went, but to Kate Kerrigan that was not necessarily true.

"The more we carry between here and Kansas, the more difficult the journey in a small wagon pulled by a broken down horse. It is said that the trail between the East and the Northwest is littered with chairs and tables and chests of drawers, even pianos. Things travelers set out with and then discovered were too cumbersome to go on with. It's best we go with no furniture at all, just bedrolls to sleep in along the way."

She saw disappointed faces and smiled.

"Once we get to Texas, we will outfit ourselves again with new things. It's exciting to think of! New place, new home, new things of our own, and a chance at true success! Your father smiles down on us, I am sure."

"I bet he'd smile even more if we took the bed he built for me," Ivy said.

Kate smiled and shook her head.

"No, dear. He'd tell you that you could

have a new and better one once we are in Texas and running our own cattle ranch."

"Mother," Quinn said, "we're poor people and you've spent all your money on a wagon and horse."

"And a Henry rifle," Kate said. "Well used and abused but serviceable, the man who sold it to me said."

"Then how are we going to have the money to start a ranch? No one is going to loan us money for it."

"No loan will be needed," Kate said. "The same good Irishman who befriended your grandfather and brought him to America is going to befriend us again, and help settle the Kerrigans in Texas, with sufficient means to obtain shelter, land, and cattle. Though there are many cattle free for the taking out on the plains, the offspring of cattle allowed to run loose during the war years."

"Who is this man?" Quinn asked.

"His name is Hagan, Cornelius Hagan. In days past he was a wealthy man in the old country, owner of much land. He was and is a good man, devoted to Christian charity and help for the poor. His father, Lord William Hagan, was a famed and very wealthy Irish landlord. More than any other landlord on the Isle, he gave aid to his tenants when the potatoes went bad. He paid their poorhouse fees without complaint, and when the opportunity came, he did more than pay their ship's fare to America. He outfitted a ship of his own to carry them. And no leaving the voyagers to survive on nothing more than the daily ship's ration, a meager amount . . . oh no. He sent ample food to see them all well fed until they reached America."

Kate wiped Shannon's mouth free of oatmeal.

"Your father and his kin had a much easier voyage than did I and my family," she said. "Of course we were grateful for all our own English lord did for us, but I must confess that there was some aspect of leaping from the frying pan into the fire involved. We very nearly starved before we reached American shores."

"So is Lord Hagan the man we'll see in Kansas?" Quinn said.

"No, that was the *father* of the man we'll see. Lord William Hagan is no longer living. His son, Cornelius, still lives, and left our homeland to build a new life for himself in America. It was he who befriended your father in a special way, grateful to him because your father once saved the life of Mr. Hagan's sister when she was involved in a carriage and wagon accident at the edge of the Five Points in New York."

"What did Pa do?" Quinn said.

"Your father, God rest him, lifted the end of a heavy wagon to allow the poor woman, who had been cast from the carriage and fallen beneath the wagon, to be pulled free. He was a strong man, your father, and willing to involve himself in help to others. Which is why we in turn are blessed with help when we need it."

"I'm not sure it is a good thing to take charity, Mother," said Quinn.

"Had you had more time to know your father, you would have learned a lesson from him regarding that very matter, son. He had a saying he'd been taught by his grandfather: A wise man knows when to give aid, and when to accept it, for there is no shame in either. The right thinking for us regarding what Mr. Hagan will do for us is simply one of gratitude, and a determination to be just as helpful to others as he is to us."

"But he's rich. We're poor," said Ivy. "How can we help anyone?"

"Another saying: It is oft true that the most valuable help is that which comes not from the purse but from the hand and the heart."

Quinn rolled his eyes. Still a boy as he was, he'd no love of Irish sayings and his mother knew hundreds of them.

"How do we know this man will help us?"

"Your father stayed in contact with Mr. Hagan through the years. Mr. Hagan is a dreamer of big dreams, and saw your father as a man with the heart and ability to help him carry them out. He intended to build success for himself in beef, agriculture, and railroads. And Joe told me a few times that sometimes Mr. Hagan talked of town building. Creating settlements across the country, linking them by good roads, and particularly by railroads. As I said, he is a dreamer of big dreams. He told your father that whenever he was ready, he would provide the backing for a ranching enterprise on the plains of western Texas. There was even mention of a town that would be named Kerrigan."

"After father?"

"Yes. Your father would operate the ranch, make a fortune for himself and for Mr. Hagan, and a town would grow up and bear your father's name."

"But Papa has been dead for five years now," Quinn said. "Why do you think this Hagan fellow would still be willing to throw money our way when the man he counted on to carry out his plan is already dead and gone?"

"I have had some correspondence of my own with Mr. Hagan since your father's passing. His plans and dreams are unchanged. He believes that those of us who remain, bearing your father's name as our own, have the ability to do what Joe is no longer here to do."

Ivy looked perplexed. "Ma, are you saying that a man believes that you, a woman, could develop and operate a cattle ranch?"

"Not just a ranch, dear. An entire cattle empire, run by the family of Joseph Kerrigan, with initial backing from the Hagan fortune, and perhaps help along the way if it is needed. It is my plan that no such help be required. Any operation with the Kerrigan name on it should be self-supporting, and able to grow on its own. That is *my* dream, as it was your father's."

"Will Trace be with us, Mother?" asked Shannon in her small little voice.

"He will, dear. Arrangements have been made for us to meet him along the way. By the time we have reached Texas and work begins on our ranch, Trace will be almost a man grown and he'll shoulder most of the work we do. As will you, Quinn."

"And the rest of us, too?" Ivy asked.

"All of us, child. All of us."

Ivy crossed her arms over her chest and gave one of her typical frowns. "I don't know that I want to be a ranch family."

"Want to be rich?" asked her twin brother. "Want to be able to go into the town of Kerrigan and buy yourself the best dresses in the shops? Then someday get married to a rich cattleman and live like that the rest of your life?"

Kate Kerrigan chuckled. "I think there may be more than one dreamer of big dreams in this room."

"I want to go," Shannon said, her wan face showing more color than it had in many months. Her coughing was mostly gone, and when she did cough, it lacked the wracking, wince-inducing quality it had once possessed. "How will we get to Texas, Mother? And do we have to go to Kansas first?"

"Most of our journey will be on a better, larger wagon provided to us by Mr. Hagan," Kate said. "We will receive that wagon in Kansas, where he lives. The town is called —"

"Let me guess," Quinn said. "Hagan."

"You are right, son — nearly. Haganville, to be more precise."

"Big rich man, stooping down to help the poor weak Irish — I don't like it, Mother."

223

"Quinn, Mr. Hagan is as Irish as we are. And he is helping us because your father helped him rescue a sister he loved."

"Are you sure this is all really going to happen, Ma?"

"I have no reason to think otherwise," Kate said. "Because I'll make it happen."

"I don't want to go," Ivy said.

"We have to do things we don't want sometimes, Ivy. Trace doesn't want to be hiding out sleeping in some woodshed because he's been wrongly accused. We'll be together and we'll make an adventure of it, just like your father would have wanted."

"Can he see us, Mama?" asked Shannon.

"I believe he can," Kate replied. "And I think he'll be traveling with us every step of the way."

Quinn made a little snorting sound and wished Trace was around.

Trace lived in the real world, not in a land of make-believe.

Chapter Twenty-Five

As towns went, this one was nothing to remember, a settlement perched at the ragged edge of nowhere with little past and no future.

Its single dusty street lined with a few stores, a saloon and some scattered shacks, no one was glad at Trace Kerrigan's coming and no one would regret his leaving.

Riding an old but half-decent mare he'd gained through some itinerant farm labor in Kentucky on a meandering route to Missouri, he plodded through and cast uninterested glances around, trying to find something worth looking at.

In this dismal little place he felt a long way from home.

It was almost enough to make him rethink his assumptions about the world west of the Mississippi River. Like many Americans, Trace held a somewhat romanticized view of the expansion of the nation farther and farther into the western frontier — but if this little bit of nothing was typical of what one found in the West, maybe there were some wrongly exalted notions floating around the national consciousness.

And just as he thought that, he saw her, and suddenly the town didn't seem so dismal.

A girl, who looked at first and second glance to be about the same age as himself, grinned at him from the lantern-lighted porch of the mean little saloon, a timber structure with a low false front and shingle roof.

Her dress was too short at the bottom and too low at the top, and her hair had a spilled-out style that spoke of saloons and dance halls and rough living — but she was staring at him brazenly, her smile unwavering.

She flounced out from her standing place and crossed the street toward him. "Hey, young feller!"

"Ma'am."

"What the — what's this 'ma'am' nonsense? I doubt I'm a day older than you are, handsome!"

Truth was, Trace couldn't tell how old she was.

She had that quality about her common

to females who took the wrong path in life. The old ones tried to face-paint their way back to youth again, and the young ones tried to look older and worldly.

Trace doubted this gal, whatever her age, had any notion he was only fifteen. For all he knew she might be fifteen herself, or fifteen years beyond that.

"You looking for some company tonight, sparkles?"

Sparkles? He gave her a quizzical look. What kind of name was that to call a man?

"I'm just heading west to meet my kinfolk," Trace said. "Looking for a town called Haganville."

"Well then, I thought you and me might have some fun, sparkles. Cost you though."

"That ain't my name," Trace said.

"Then what is? Mine's Erlean."

"Mine's my own business. Good evening to you, Ma'am, Miss Erlean, or whatever you want to be called."

"You're no fun at all, sparkles. I'd say you got the look of the preacher about you, if'n it wasn't for the hog leg you're carrying."

"I'm surely not a preacher, but you're right about one thing. I'm no fun. Good night."

He rode on past. The woman glowered at him, then returned to her place on the saloon porch.

He heard her holler after him.

"You ain't nothing but a boy, anyhow! I don't need no boy! A woman like me needs a man! A real one!"

"Hope you find one in this town," Trace called back, grinning.

Trace had but seventy-five cents left in his pocket and halfway out to a little general store on the edge of town where he hoped to buy some crackers and cheese, he rode past a stagecoach station. A bonfire burned on the station grounds, a beacon in the night for late-arriving passengers.

A tall man wearing batwing chaps and a wide-brimmed, battered hat stood by the fire warming his hands since the night had turned cool. Scarlet light played along the front of the man's lean form like blood on a blade.

Trace pegged the man as a one of the Kansas cattle drovers he'd heard so much about recently, but hungry, he tried to hurry his mare a little, but she was having none of it.

He didn't blame the horse. He'd arrived in town after hours of fruitless searching for Haganville, wearying her unnecessarily.

"Hey, hold up young feller," the drover said.

Trace drew rein and waited, the Colt in his waistband a reassuring weight.

"You made a smart move back there, feller," the man said.

Trace turned as the man stepped toward him. He wore spurs that chimed with every step and carried a holstered Colt on his waist, high, in the style of a horseman.

"Hi," Trace said. "Is there anything I can do for you?"

"For me, not a thing. But I can do something for you."

The drover smiled, showing good teeth.

"Didn't mean to surprise you," he said. "Sorry about that."

"Didn't hurt me any." Trace stuck his hand. "Kerrigan. Trace Kerrigan."

The man shook Trace's hand. His palm felt as rough as a piece of broken sandstone. This was a man who knew work and had known it for years.

"Kerrigan, did you say? Why hell, this world's getting smaller all the time. That's the name of a family I was sent out here to meet at the stage station. This burg is called Benson and Haganville is about ten miles farther up the trail."

"That'd be my family. I'm meeting them in Haganville. We've kind of been separated by circumstances for a while now. How did you know we were coming?" Trace said.

"I didn't. But Mr. Hagan sent a wire all the way to Nashville. He said not to send a reply, so he don't know if your ma got it or not."

The drover grinned.

"If she gets here, she got it. If she don't, she didn't. Name's Brock Davis and I've been riding for Mr. Hagan since the war ended. Do I hear a bit of Irish in your talk, Trace?"

"You might. I was born and raised in these United States, but my parents were Irish. Shouldn't say 'were,' though, for it's only my father who is gone. My mother is still living."

"Name's Kate, I think?"

"That's right." For a moment Trace felt worried. Might the trouble he'd fled in Tennessee have anything to do with this man being here, knowing his family and waiting for them?

"Mr. Hagan is Irish like you, except he was actually born over there. He's a man of great wealth, and he's real interested in your family, Trace. The plan was for me to meet them and take them to a place to stay at. Then the boss wants to meet the entire family. Of course I didn't expect to see you riding in here on that mare all alone."

"Must be a fine thing to have a town named after you," Trace said, hoping to change the subject of why he was traveling apart from his family.

"Aw, I don't know. A town name don't buy a man a loaf of bread or a swallow of coffee. Mr. Hagan's a big and powerful man, but he ain't high and mighty like some I could name. That's the best way for a man to be, rich or poor."

"Can I ask you something, Mr. Davis?"

"Only if you call me Brock. Mister never set well with me."

"All right, Brock. What were you talking about earlier when you said I made a wise decision?"

"Oh, about Erlean?"

"Yes, her."

"Well, there's a feller hereabouts goes by the name of Charlie Palmer. A big feller is Charlie and good with the Colt. Some says he's killed seven men, others say nine, but I know for a fact he's killed three hombres over Erlean."

"He's jealous?" Trace said.

"Jealous ain't much of a word when it comes to Charlie. If he catches anybody sparkin' Erlean, he goes stark, raving mad and it usually ends up with a dead man on the saloon floor, his beard in the sawdust."

"Sparking a girl? Is that why she called me sparkles?"

"Could be."

"I don't want Charlie's girl and if I see him I'll tell him that."

"Well, he ain't a man who listens to reason," Davis said. "Charlie shoots first and regrets it later."

"Then I've had a narrow escape," Trace said.

"Charlie ain't in town right now, so you were pretty safe. But my advice to you, being new to the west an' all, is to avoid sporting gals. They're bad for your health."

"I'll keep that in mind," Trace said.

"Best climb down," Davis said. "I reckon we might have a wait ahead of us."

Trace saw a moment's hesitation in the drover's eyes.

Finally the man said, "You meet up with any Indian trouble on the trail?"

Trace shook his head. "No, I sure didn't."

Davis seemed relieved.

"That's good to hear. The Comanche have been playing hob, killed a settler and his family a week ago ten miles east of here."

"I wish you hadn't told me that," Trace said.

"You should know."

Trace nodded.

"Yes, I guess I should."

And now he was really worried.

The stage station beacon fire still burned brightly, but the old Indian man whose job it was to keep it tended was snoring on the station porch, loudly enough that neither Trace nor Brock Davis heard the approach of the two riders until it was too late.

"Good evening to you, amigos!" the biggest of the pair said, his pistol out and leveled.

He'd just ridden around from the rear of the station and at his side was a smaller man, shifty-eyed and nervous, though his gun was steady enough. He had a wide, pointless grin and looked to Trace that he was tetched in the head.

"Hello, Señor Davis," said the bigger man. "How convenient to have run into so generous an hombre as you just at the time Pablo and me are short of funds."

"I'm flat broke, Julio," Davis said. "You'll need to go find somebody else."

"Well! Once again I learn something from my good friend Señor Davis. He is broke, he says, yet his compadre carries a fine revolver in his pants."

Davis waved a hand at the bandits.

"Trace, please allow me to introduce you

to this pair of beauties. They're breeds, half-Comanche, half-Mexican and all border trash."

Davis grinned.

"They may be dressed like vaqueros, but the only cattle they've ever herded were stolen."

"Ah, that is so true," the man called Julio said. "But we are still poor men and that makes me very sad. If we had guns and horses we could sell them and buy mescal and that would make Julio and his cousin Miguel ver' happy."

"Miguel, please put away that damned pistol," Davis said. "You're making me nervous the way you're waving it around. Julio, your cousin's got no business aiming a gun at anybody. He's too crazy in the head."

"No, no, no, Señor Brock. We don't put away our guns, no. We hold them on you so you will be wise and give us what we ask of you. That is how the bandit business works, señor."

Davis glanced over at Trace. "Sorry we had to run into these two here. We're old acquaintances, these two fools and me. I got lead into Miguel a year back, caught him and Julio rustling our beeves over to Lost Creek. Only winged him though, more's the pity."

"That is a thing Miguel does not forget," the small man said, his mouth twitching.

Without warning, the revolver in Miguel's hand stabbed orange flame in the darkness.

Brock grunted and jerked and blood spattered from the underside of his left forearm.

"That is where you shot me, señor," Miguel said, grinning. "An eye for an eye."

"I figgered you out fer a rat and low down, Miguel," Brock said. "Now I know fer sure."

"I . . . I sorry, Señor Brock," the breed said. "The eye for an eye is necessary, you understand? The Bible says so. A holy father told me that."

"Put the gun away before it happens again," Brock said to Miguel. "For old time's sake, I don't want to kill you, but if I have to I will."

Julio thumbed back the hammer of his Colt.

"No more games and big boasting Señor Brock," he said. "No bad wound, that one. No bad hurt. Now you take out your gun, slow, slow, and let it drop to the ground."

Brock two-fingered his gun from the holster and let it thud to the dirt.

"Ver' good," Julio said, grinning. He showed several gold teeth. "Now I want your horse, your fine rifle and your watch and chain. Oh and I want the silver ring you wear on your little finger."

"It's a gambler's ring, Julio," Davis said. "It's of no use to you."

"Maybe I will play poker on the steamboats one day," the breed said. He shrugged. "Or I can sell it."

Brock glanced over at Trace, who thus far had been silent throughout the confrontation.

"My gun's on the ground, Trace, and we're finished," he said.

"That is so, Brock," Julio said. "It is so sad for you."

The breed swung his revolver and covered Trace.

"Now bring over your fine American stud or I'll shoot the boy right out of his saddle."

"He's out of it, Julio," Davis said. "I'll get the hoss."

The big drover sent Trace a single look, a significant appeal that managed somehow to convey just what he wanted the younger man to do.

Trace, smart as a whip, instantly understood.

He drew the Colt from his waistband and deftly flipped it over to Brock, who just as deftly caught it.

Trace rolled from the saddle as Julio fired.

The breed's ball passed a foot above the young man's head as Trace slammed into the ground.

Davis had the revolver in his fist. He fired at Julio. A hit. Fired again.

Julio shrieked and threw up his arms, his gun spinning away from him.

He tumbled from the saddle, shot in the forehead and in the chest, dead when he hit the ground.

The watch in Davis's vest barely ticked two seconds between Julio's shot and the drover's answering fire.

And for the first time in his life, Trace saw what a skilled pistolero like Davis could do with a six-gun. It was a lesson he never forgot.

"Drop it, Miguel," Davis said in dead cold voice. "Or by God, I'll kill you right where you're at."

Miguel screamed and jerked wildly on his mount's reins and the horse pranced a full-circle turn. When the breed faced Davis again and tried to level his revolver.

"No, Miguel!" Davis yelled.

The breed dropped his hand and let his Colt hang by his side.

"Trace, there's a piggin string in my saddlebags over there. Use it to tie Miguel's hands to the saddle horn. Oh, and take his gun away from him while you're at it."

Trace had no idea what a piggin string was, but he found a length of looped rope in the bag and figured that had to be it.

He stepped to Miguel, took his revolver, then tied the breed's wrists to the saddle horn.

"Miguel, it was fun chasing after you and Julio when you'd rustled a cow or two," he said. "But the fun ended right here tonight. If I see you again around these parts I'll kill you."

"Yes, señor. I understand."

Miguel looked scared.

"You stay out of trouble now, or you'll end up like your cousin, dead on a dirt street at the far end of nowhere," Davis said.

He let out a yell as he slapped Miguel's horse on the rump.

The breed rocked and jolted into the night, his hands firmly bound to the saddle horn.

Davis shook his head.

"Miguel is not a bad hombre, as breeds go, but he's none too smart. That's why Julio was able to control him and steer him wrong."

"Brock, how did you ever learn to use a gun like that?" Trace said.

"It took years, a war, a heap of shooting

scrapes, and a lot of dead men."

The drover's eyes were bleak.

"I hope you never have the need to learn the way of the Colt like I did."

But the older man's eyes held a warning that the need might one day arrive . . . and that Trace would have to learn almighty sudden.

Chapter Twenty-Six

"How's your arm?" Trace said. "I think you best see a doctor."

"There's no doctor in this town or for fifty miles around," Davis said. "But our ranch cook does some doctoring and mighty good at it he is, too."

"You're bleeding," Trace said.

"It's fine. Miguel's ball barely grazed the skin. I'm not even going to bother bandaging it. Hey, this Colt of yours has a balance like I never felt in a gun. Hardly any recoil at all."

"Yeah, it was a gift from one of the best gunsmiths there ever was. Down in Tennessee. He put it together custom, worked on it for weeks."

"Well, here it is back, and thanks for the use of it. That's a revolver any man would be proud to have."

Trace took back the gun and shoved it into his waistband.

"I'm glad I met you, Brock," he said.

"And the feeling is mutual, I'm sure. I'm a man you're going to get to know real well over the next few months."

Davis nodded to Julio's body.

"We'll drag that over to the stage depot porch there. No point in him laying around upsetting folks."

When the job was done, Davis prodded the ancient Indian asleep on his chair on the porch.

"Well I be damned," he said. "We got another one to put away. This old Chippewa ain't sleeping. He's dead."

So they put the old Indian under the porch, too, beside Julio.

The Kerrigan wagon rolled into town three days later.

Trace smiled when he saw Quinn up on the driver's seat beside Kate. He held the old .44 Henry and by his intent face took his job as guard seriously.

The reunion was one between a group of very weary people. Trace was tired from long riding and from the unexpected violent adventures of the night since he'd met Brock Davis, and the balance of the Kerrigans were each exhausted in the way that only a wagon ride on rough trails can make one.

Trace was glad to see Shannon looking brighter and healthier than she had in many months. She was surprisingly vigorous as well, bouncing along with the level of energy youngsters of her age were supposed to have, but which she never had. She bounded up to Trace and shoved her beloved doll, Kate, up at him.

"Katie wants to kiss you, Trace!" she said, giggling.

Trace, playing along with a forced good nature he was actually too tired to really be feeling, leaned his cheek down and let Shannon press the doll's yellow-cloth face against his cheek while Shannon made a loud smooching noise with her lips. "Oh!" she said then. "Katie says your whiskers are scratchy!"

"And who is this fine young lass?" Brock boomed out, approaching Shannon and Trace with a big grin on his face.

"Brock, this is my youngest sister, Shannon. Shannon, meet my new friend, Mr. Davis."

"You can just call me Mr. Brock, if that's easier to remember," he said. "Brock is my first name."

"Okay, Mr. Brock." Shannon shoved her

rag doll up toward Brock as she had toward Trace moments earlier. "This is Katie, Mr. Brock. She's my best friend."

"Well . . . hello, Katie," Brock said. "I'm very pleased to meet you."

"Katie kissed Trace but she won't kiss you because she doesn't know you yet, and because your whiskers would be even scratchier than Trace's. He's only fifteen years old, you see."

Brock nodded and Shannon skipped away to go examine the dancing fire.

"You really only fifteen?"

"Yep. I'm told I look older than my age."

"You do. How old would you say I am?" Brock asked.

"I don't know. Thirty-five?"

"Add four years to that and you'll have it. I guess I look younger than my age then."

Niall walked up. "Trace, there's men under the porch of this place. Two of 'em, just laying there. And they smell kind of bad."

"Just pay them no mind, Niall," Trace said. "They're not hurting anybody."

"They sleeping?"

"That's right. Sound asleep, both of them. They'll sleep the night through, and then some."

■ ■ ■ ■

The first night of the reunited Kerrigans was spent in a hotel one town past the humble one Trace had found so uninteresting.

A surprisingly spacious accommodation, the hotel provided a much-needed night's respite from travel exhaustion.

Kate had trouble falling asleep because her mind kept replaying the dangers and hardships of the trail.

They'd met a cavalry lieutenant returning to his post at Fort Ellsworth the afternoon the Comanche rode so close to their wagon she smelled their horses and saw the red, white, or yellow paint that decorated the hair partings of both men and women.

Kate sent the children into the back of the wagon and took the Henry from Quinn.

"Will they attack us, Lieutenant Werner?" she said.

She was surprised and a little irritated that the young soldier sat his horse so calmly.

"If they were going to attack us, they'd have done it by now, Mrs. Kerrigan," Werner said. "Comanche are mighty notional."

"Why do they ride so close to my wagon?"

Kate said.

"To let you know that they're aware of you."

"Well, Lieutenant, I'm certainly aware of them," Kate said.

"This band is going somewhere," Werner said. "The young warriors are in the lead, the women of childbearing age behind them, all mounted. Those that are passing now are the old people, and they walk. The Comanche don't set much store by old timers, especially men."

"Why not?" Kate said, peering into the dust cloud kicked up by hooves and human feet.

"Well, it's a disgrace for a Comanche warrior to grow old," the lieutenant said. "It means they were not brave enough in battle." He smiled. "In the world of the Comanche only cowards don't die young."

"Look, who is that crowd of people being whipped along by boys? Jesus, Mary, and Joseph, I see a white face or two among them."

"Slaves," Werner said. "Comanche slaves always bring up the rear of the column."

"But the white people . . ." Kate said, horrified.

Werner's face was empty of emotion, displaying a professional soldier's stoicism.

245

"White slaves don't last long," he said. "Unlike Mexicans and other Indian captives."

"But —"

"There's nothing we can do for them, Mrs. Kerrigan."

"Can you talk to them, Lieutenant?"

"Sure I could, with a regiment of cavalry and a battery of cannon behind me."

"Then it's a pitiful sight," Kate said.

Werner nodded.

"Remember it well, Mrs. Kerrigan, for you may never see its like again."

Kate finally slept and lay abed until late morning, a thing she'd never done before in her life.

But her qualms of conscience vanished when she and the children enjoyed a fine breakfast in the hotel dining room, served on a long, broad table covered in snow-white linen.

"If this is an example of the hospitality of Mr. Hagan, I think we are going to find ourselves enjoying this journey more than we might have expected," she said.

She picked up a piece of bacon on her fork and held it suspended between plate and mouth, lost in thought.

Finally she said, "I find myself more and

more curious about the man. Such a level of effort on our behalf, and welcome, and hospitality. Could there be some motive beyond his gratitude toward Joseph in all this?"

"Do you know what I think, Ma?" Trace said. "I think he's doing this because he really believes in what he has set us to doing. He's sure we Kerrigans can create our own empire in Texas in the cattle trade."

"Your son is right," said Brock Davis said, who was seated near Trace and Kate, and having difficulty keeping his eyes off the vivid beauty of the latter.

"Once you get to know Mr. Hagan you'll understand all this better, see that it fits with his manner and his way of doing things. The Cornelius Hagan I know is a gentleman through and through and I would have been surprised had he *not* extended such a level of welcome and support for you."

"He must be quite an extraordinary man," Kate said.

"Extraordinary indeed, Ma'am."

"And what will be your role in this, once you have delivered us to our most singular benefactor?"

"I will be your wagon master, Ma'am. Since it is well known to me, I will scout the trail that takes you to your new home in Texas."

"Will I be able to start the building of my home before the winter sets in?" Kate said.

"You'll find that that won't be necessary. That task is in progress already, even as we speak here this morning. The boss sent builders ahead to start work on a cabin for you and the children. It will be small, but it will be the start of something grander, I'm sure."

"It will be," Kate said. "Of that I am certain."

CHAPTER TWENTY-SEVEN

The house that was home to Cornelius Hagan was very much more than the usual plains cabin.

It stood on the flatlands of Kansas like some medieval palace, lifting its towers and spires toward the heavens and giving silent voice to the unquestionable wealth behind it. As Kate Kerrigan first saw the Hagan mansion her thoughts turned inward, back to that fateful day Joe had the courage and will to lift a wagon off an injured woman.

The young Irishman's good deed — and strength — had set the wheels in motion that led to this very day. She thought that if only Joe could be here to share in this grand adventure with their children it would make her happiness complete.

Kate rode in one of the private carriages that had arrived at the hotel where the reunited Kerrigans had spent their first night.

Two four-wheelers drawn by strong horses and driven by expert coachmen had carried the family across gently rolling grass country with occasional oak and hickory trees.

Trace was the only Kerrigan not in a carriage, opting instead to stay in the saddle, as he had grown accustomed to riding since his flight from Nashville.

From the hotel the journey had seemed swift and easy, and the astonishing mansion and nearby town of Haganville had come into view sooner than Kate had expected.

As she gazed out the window at the place to which the carriages were taking them, her daughter Ivy spoke to her from the facing seat. "He sure admires you, Ma."

"Who are you speaking of, dear?"

"Mr. Davis. He cares for you. I can see it in how he looks at you."

"Oh, Ivy, if I believed that every man who looked at me in the way that so many do actually cared for me, I would live in a confusing world indeed. Perhaps he is taken with me at some level — that has been the case with many a man I've known. But that is far from him caring for me in any notable way."

"I don't know, Mother. I've seen other men look at you, and watch you because you are pretty, and whisper to each other about you. But Mr. Davis is different. There is more to it with him. I think he may be falling in love with you."

Kate laughed. The romantic evaluations of a nine-year-old girl . . . what value or true insight could they have? True, she herself had detected a certain intensity in the way he looked at her and spoke to her . . . but . . .

No. It was silly. A child's imagination and a child's chatter.

As the carriage steadily neared Hagan-wood, though, Kate couldn't help but turn the matter backward and evaluate it from her own perspective. What did she think of Brock Davis?

He was a fine looking man in a rugged, weathered, very western kind of way. Dark hair with a few traces of gray beginning to touch the temples and the fine dragoon mustache he was obviously so proud of. His neck was sturdy and powerfully set on a pair of broad and muscled shoulders. He was a man of strength, no doubt of it. Quite an attractive gentleman of plains and trail — this was how he struck her.

Was she attracted to him? She had to admit that in a small way the answer was yes.

But taking that attraction seriously, believing it held any meaning or prospect for future growth, that was entirely another matter.

She had to admit to herself, though, that she had been pleased to hear that Brock Davis would guide their journey to Texas.

He would be a capable guide and was good with a gun. Of that she was sure.

Whether his status might grow into something beyond that was a question only time could answer. She'd never given serious thought to being partnered with any other man than Joseph Kerrigan, who still held her heart and devotion, but now from the far side of the grave.

Such thoughts were brushed aside when the carriages at last entered the arched entrance into the inner yard of the mansion grounds, and came to a stop on a fine cobbled driveway.

The coachmen descended from their seats and stood in almost militaristic rigid fashion beside their lathered coach horses.

As the carriage doors were opened by footmen who had moved out from the mansion into the drive, Kate was suddenly conscious of the age and shabbiness of her dress, and the well-worn, tattered look of her children's clothes.

Against the backdrop of such a fine place,

the Kerrigans looked exactly like what they were: an impoverished Irish family, more fit for the potato farm or the thatch field than the parlor and sitting room.

She remembered one of her husband's favored sayings, "Keep your dignity and forget your pride."

There was a difference between the two, he had always maintained. Kate had never been certain she grasped that, but now she thought she might.

Blinking in the bright day, she held herself tall and straight and reminded herself that she was a woman of admired beauty, never mind what kind of garb she was in.

And surely, if he was any kind of sensible and worldly man at all, Hagan would hold no expectation that guests who were at the end of a long journey from a city hundreds of miles away would be anything but disheveled, uncombed, and grubby.

She brushed some dust off her dress, bucked up, smiled, and readied herself to make the best of things, however they went.

"It's very grand, this house, isn't it, Ma?" Ivy said.

"Indeed it is," Kate said. "Very grand."

"Will our new house in Texas look like this one?"

Kate laughed.

"Lordy, child, I very much doubt it."

"But it will, one day, huh?"

"Yes," Kate said. "One day it will. Only grander, with four columns out front and a huge stable to house our coaches and four."

Kate and the children were guided forward by dignified domestics and steered through an ornate door and down a mahogany lined corridor.

Trace, hat in hand, trailed behind them, staring at the pictures on the walls.

Ivy was breathless, excited, Shannon big-eyed and openmouthed. Niall tried to look in all directions at once and Quinn was solemn, like some junior statesman come to visit a rich potentate.

Brock Davis had shed his gun belt at the door and walked in with the family.

He was utterly at ease, clearly having made this pilgrimage many times before. For the Kerrigans it was something very near to being called in to meet royalty. For Brock, it was just another day in the service of his boss, who happened to be an extraordinarily wealthy man.

By the time they reached the doorway beyond which lay the broad, plush office of Cornelius Hagan, Kate had put aside her doubts regarding the family's readiness to meet the mysterious man who had so changed their lives.

And she was still anxious to know the reason for such generosity and royal treatment, as though she was Queen Victoria come to tea.

The doors opened and Kate and the children were ushered into a huge study that smelled of wood polish and more faintly of cattle.

The desk behind which Hagan sat, his head lowered as he studied a ledger, very nearly matched the expanse of the big table where the Kerrigans had dined recently in the hotel.

The carpet was a deep dark red and the heavy, mahogany furniture gleamed like port wine in a glass. A gun rack took up part of one wall and above that a painting of charging buffalo.

"Sir?" a man who appeared to be a butler said to the distracted Hagan. "The Kerrigans are here."

Hagan lifted his gray head and smiled.

Kate stared at the man behind the desk, who stared back at her in turn, intently, obviously liking what he saw.

Hagan, wearing dusty range clothes, extended a hand.

"I'm so very glad to see you here, Mrs. Kerrigan. And your fine family."

"And glad I am to be here," Kate said. Despite her shock, she added, "May I have a chair?"

Hagan looked stricken.

"Why of course you can," he said. "How remiss of me."

A flunky immediately supplied an armchair for Kate and she sat gratefully.

"Mr. Hagan, I have many questions to ask, but first let me say that you bear a strong resemblance to my late husband."

Hagan smiled. "Do I indeed?"

"Yes, you do. When I first saw your face it was . . . well, a shock."

"Am I so ugly then?" Hagan said.

Now it was Kate's turn to smile.

"No, not at all. It was the resemblance that so shocked me."

"Well, we both hail from old Ireland and perhaps back in the mists of time a Kerrigan and a Hagan could have gotten together in the light of the moon under a greenwood tree."

"That could well be the case," Kate said.

Hagan hesitated a moment and sorted out the words in his head.

Then he said, "Mrs. Kerrigan, you catch me at a bad moment since I'm occupied with business matters. But rest assured, I have only the good of you and your family at heart."

"That is indeed good to know," Kate said.

"My house is your house, so please relax and enjoy yourself. Do as you please, and if you need anything my servants will assist you."

"Thank you," Kate said. "You make us feel very welcome."

"You are welcome, and we will speak again tomorrow."

Hagan lifted his steel pen and smiled.

"Until tomorrow then," he said.

CHAPTER TWENTY-EIGHT

For the Kerrigan children, the lodgings in which they were housed for the night, rooms along an entire hallway that was theirs alone, the experience was beyond their wildest fancies of grandeur.

That the hallway and rooms were in fact merely an unused stretch of servant quarters was completely lost on youngsters who were used to shared, cramped rooms, and roofs that often leaked in the rain.

The plain, utilitarian rooms with their army cot beds and undecorated linens were to the younger Kerrigans the epitome of luxury.

No sharing of beds, no toenail scratches inflicted by a flailing fellow sleeper, no snoring from someone else's throat and nose . . . nothing could be finer, no sleep more satisfying.

When morning came and sunlight filled the rooms, the children were loathe to rise and give up the most blissful night they ever had enjoyed.

From elsewhere in the big house, though, the scent of cooking sausages floated through, enticing the reluctant risers out of their blankets at last.

Kate had slept not in a humble servant room, but in a guest bedroom the center-piece of which was a tall, canopied bed that to her looked worthy of a queen's sleeping chamber.

She had slept little, though. Her mind had been too busy trying to accommodate astonishing things she had learned in a lengthy conversation with her host, a man the sight of whom had stricken her as no other sight ever had.

He had come to her room in the wee hours of the morning, still in his range clothes, and told her what she needed to know.

As he stood at the door to leave, he hesitated.

"I had thought to leave what I'd told you until tomorrow, but I reconsidered and thought it of the greatest moment that I tell you tonight," Hagan said.

"And for that I am eternally grateful," Kate said, sitting in her old, worn robe.

She now possessed an understanding that

she'd not had before, answers to questions that could only have come from Cornelius Hagan's own lips.

Yet it all seemed so amazing, so impossible, that she simply couldn't shake off the feeling that she might close her eyes in this place and open them again to find herself back in her old widow's bed in Nashville, alone, or even on a rag heap on the floor of an unventilated Five Points tenement.

When she did awaken, though, she was still in the Hagan mansion. The bed and magnificent chamber was real, and the rank foulness of Five Points was a thousand miles and a lifetime away.

She rose and wrapped herself in her robe she removed from a closet the size of her old Nashville bedroom.

Following the same delicious odors that had drawn her children, she made her way to the dining hall where breakfast was being served.

Sausages, eggs, fruits, a variety of breads, jams, flavored butters . . . never had such a breakfast been laid before her.

"We will reach Texas as fat as pigs!" Kate said, drawing laughter from her children.

"Maybe we can just curl our fat selves up into balls and roll all the way down to Texas," suggested Niall.

Kate smiled at her youngest son and tapped his forehead. "The intelligence of this family you are, Niall."

"I know that, Mother. I've always known that."

Trace and Quinn joined in the laughter of the others, but only fleetingly. Their manner and whispered conversation was of a more serious variety.

"The others are too young to remember well enough to have noticed," Trace said. "But you and me, and certainly Ma did . . . she saw it clear."

"I know I did," Quinn said. "He doesn't really look like Father — yet he does. So much so around his eyes that it's almost like seeing pa himself. I caught myself wondering for a moment if somehow it really *was* him. That maybe he hadn't died after all, and had gained all this wealth somehow. Then I knew it couldn't be."

"I had the same kinds of thoughts, and I think Ma must have, too, which is why she looked the way she did. And needed that chair in a hurry. The shock of it."

"Trace, I know it can't be him, but how do you explain it? It can't just be some accident that they are so alike."

"I can't explain it, Quinn. But maybe Brock Davis knows something."

"Let's make a pact, Trace: we're going to figure this out. Whatever answer there is to find, we'll find it."

Under the table, the brothers quickly shook hands, and then returned to their breakfasts.

There had been no anticipation on the part of the Kerrigans that they would remain for any extended period at the Hagan mansion before launching their southward odyssey to Texas.

Factors related to their preparations, though, intervened.

Two wagons were being constructed by a top-quality wagon builder to transport them on the journey, and problems with wheels delayed the work.

Also, one of the drivers recruited and hired for the journey suffered a failure of the heart and died, and it took extra time to hire a replacement.

The delays prompted no complaints from the youngsters of the family, who luxuriated in the unfamiliar opulence around them.

Kate worried privately that they would become spoiled by the easy living, less fit than they would have been to make the arduous trek across southern Kansas and then through the Nations.

Even when they crossed the Texas border there would still be many miles farther to go before they reached the place where Hagan had already planned the ranch the Kerrigans would operate on his behalf.

Kate worried but did not dwell on it.

She would not deny her children this opportunity to live in a way they might never encounter again.

Even if her fondest dreams of building a successful Texas empire were realized, at its best it was unlikely to match the splendor of the Hagan mansion and the life lived by its founder and master.

The town of Haganville provided further pleasure for the Kerrigans.

There were stores and markets aplenty, and dealers in guns and horses and domestic goods.

In this town Trace could roam openly and freely, with none of the hiding that had become part of his later Nashville days.

It was walking with their mother on one of the boardwalks of Haganville that Quinn and Trace approached their mother about the mystery surrounding Cornelius Hagan.

"Ma, me and Trace are old enough to remember pa's face quite well. Mr. Hagan looks very like him, don't you think?"

"Yes, I do, very striking."

Trace said, "So we're telling you nothing you don't already know. In fact you were the first to notice it. But there are things we think you know that we don't."

"You mean the reason for the resemblance?" Kate said.

She was not surprised by the question and had been anticipating it sooner even than it had come.

"There is a reason," she said. "But I have to leave you disappointed. I'm not free to tell it to you. In time I think you will know, probably from Mr. Hagan himself. Until then, I can only leave you in frustration, and I'm sorry. I can tell you only that the resemblance you see is real, and has a reason. I can't yet tell you what that reason is, since Mr. Hagen wishes to keep it secret for the moment."

Kate smiled. "Forgive me, boys. I only wish I could ease your curiosity right away."

"But Ma . . ."

"Leave it be, Quinn," Trace said. "When she is free to do so, Ma will tell us. Or maybe Mr. Hagan will."

And so the matter was dropped and allowed to lie dormant.

Trace, with the advantage of a year's maturity over Quinn, was able to accept the lack of understanding with less frustration than his little brother.

Quinn kept asking the same questions for a while, but eventually lost himself in the plans for their impending departure.

The deceased driver was replaced, horses and saddles obtained for the travelers, and the wagons outfitted.

Brock Davis was allowed to hire two Texas gun hands to accompany them for added security.

Concern over the family furnishings that had to be abandoned when the family fled Nashville were allayed by Hagan's assurances that he would have replacement items, and better, shipped to them, and that indeed he'd already sent out a wagonload of tables, chairs, beds, and the like to the cabin under construction near the head of the Brazos River.

Contrary to expectations, given Hagan's obvious love of the flamboyant, the actual departure of the two-wagon train and its band of travelers happened without much ceremony.

Hagan saw them off, improvising a brief speech intended to inspire them while reminding them they had his support should difficulties requiring his intervention arise.

Good-byes were said, Quinn and Trace vainly hoped that their questions about

Hagan would be given answers, and Ivy bawled at having to turn her back on the luxuries of the mansion.

Oxen plodded, wheels turned, hooves tramped dirt, and wagons rolled southward toward the Nations.

The Kerrigan clan, Kate in the lead with her faithful Henry, headed for Texas.

CHAPTER TWENTY-NINE

The renegade called himself Rain Horse. His father, hung by Texas Rangers for a rapist and murderer, had been called Rains On His Horses, and his son had adapted the name and took it for his own.

He greatly venerated his dead pa.

Rain Horse, a murderous brute who stood barely five foot tall, was the terror of the Nations.

He cut a bloody swath across the territory, killing, torturing, punishing without mercy those whites he found intruding onto what he considered Indian lands.

He also raided into Texas and Kansas to plunder, rape, and kill.

To the Rangers he was a marked man, but to his followers he was a hero, a human manifestation of *Ocasta,* the dark Cherokee god who wears a stone coat and stalks the earth causing endless turmoil.

Rain Horse was small and frail, with coal

black eyes and the face of a vicious ape, and he lived life on his own terms.

He believed that, for each life he took his own vitality increased and strengthened. And the younger the slain, the greater the stolen life force for Rain Horse to enjoy.

Among his band were two white/Cherokee breeds.

The bald one was known only as Steel for his love of the machete as a weapon, the other a hulking savage who hailed from Illinois and was named Bill Bodine. Those two were the worst of the worst, as cruel, violent, and lustful as Rain Horse himself, and men even the wild Cherokee renegades who rode for him stepped around.

Rain Horse and his riders sat their ponies on the rim of a high limestone and shale ridge and stared down at the broad and slightly rolling flat.

A train of four wagons crawled along through knee-high grass, only four men armed with lever rifles to guard it.

Rain Horse glared at the moving vehicles and the people in and around the wagons.

"Looks promising to me," Bodine said to his leader. "We can have them guards down and scalped afore they know what hit them."

"There are maidens among them," Rain Horse said. "I am of a humor for maidens."

"Then I say we go get them," Bodine said.

"You forget that what you say does not matter, Bodine. It is Rain Horse who decides."

"Well, what do you say, boss?"

"We will bide our time," Rain Horse said.

It had not taken long for the journey to grow laborious.

Ivy was so annoyed by the incessant creaking of a wheel and the heavy plod of the oxen that she squeezed her hands hard over her ears and squinted her eyes closed, too, as if by blocking vision she could also eliminate noise.

But the squeaking went on.

Finally one of the hired Texas guns, noticing Ivy's distress, produced from his saddlebags a Jew's harp and set out to cover the squeaking sound with his twanging music. The harp, though, was worse than the wheel, and Ivy was more punished than ever.

Trace, riding beside Kate, flicked his eyes toward Ivy for a moment and said, "I wonder sometimes if she'll ever grow up to be nice, or just stay this ornery her whole life."

"She'll be fine," Kate said. "Give her time."

"I suppose you are right, Ma. But I could more easily listen to ten wheels squeaking than to hear Ivy wail about it."

"Patience, Trace. Patience is a cardinal virtue."

They passed into the Indian Nations with no discernible change in the landscape, a vast, ocean of grass that stretched as far as a tall man on a tall horse could see.

But day-by-day, Brock Davis's demeanor grew more somber and tense.

He constantly scanned the terrain around them, particularly the horizon, and conferred often with his hired guns, as stone-faced and wary as he was.

Kate noticed, and finally said, "Brock, are we riding into trouble?"

He was clearly hesitant to answer.

Then finally: "It may be so. I have no wish to stir fear, Mrs. Kerrigan, but this is dangerous territory. There are many bandits and renegades here, white men, Mexicans, and Indians."

He swallowed hard and abruptly stopped speaking.

"I have been scared before," Kate said. "It won't be a new experience."

"Well, Ma'am, the worst of them is a man who calls himself Rain Horse. What we don't want is to meet up with him or any of his posse. We have females with us. You understand?"

"I understand," Kate said. "I understand very well."

A chill settled on her and her eyes turned to her girls.

"I think we should have the girls ride inside one of the wagons while we're in the Nations. Keep them out of sight."

"Not a bad idea, Ma'am. In fact I reckon a very good one. Easier to guard them that way."

The girls were not eager to comply, so without specifics, Kate told them there was particular danger to females from some of the criminals who haunted the Indian Nations.

Shannon had no understanding of what her mother meant, but Ivy grasped enough to stop protesting and hide away beneath the canvas.

They moved on without incident, though Davis gave Kate a battered man's hat and she tucked her flaming hair under it.

With her womanly shape the effort did little to disguise that she was a woman. But it could work at a distance, or so she hoped.

CHAPTER THIRTY

The next day, after a tense night camped in the open, two different but equally alarming signs of trouble presented themselves to the travelers.

The first was a subtle, then blatant, shift in the weather.

The sky took on an odd, yellowish tint and the wind grew erratic, gusting then dropping again, and the air had a charged, electric feel and smelled of ozone, as though a lightning storm was close.

"We may be in for a bad time," Brock Davis told Kate and Trace. "This is prime weather for tornadoes."

"I've never seen a tornado," Kate said. "What would we do if one appears?"

Davis thought for a moment, his face troubled.

"Abandon the wagons, look for gullies or low spots to lie in, or hide ourselves among rocks if there are any to be had. Turn the oxen and horses free so they have a chance to watch out for themselves. Best thing is to hope we don't run into one in the first place."

He glanced at the sky.

"Damn it, seems like the whole world is turning yellow. This could go bad on us, or it could just blow over and break up."

Moving along, opting not to tell the younger children and give them a fright perhaps unnecessary, they kept their eyes on the sky and horizon, and constantly gauged the way the wind felt against their skin.

It was then that Kate saw something that, at a glance, looked like it might be a distant funnel cloud. A closer look, and a conference with Davis, revealed it was instead a line of rising smoke.

"What might it be from?" Kate asked.

"I hate to say what I fear it could be," Brock replied. "But I'm obliged to take the gun hands and go for a look-see."

"I guess I should I keep the Henry close, huh?" Kate said.

"You should keep it real close. Trace is here and he's capable. If you see trouble, fire three fast shots in the air. We'll hear and ride back fast."

After Davis and the Texans rode out, the

wind rose again and a strange and ominous tingling charged the atmosphere.

The canvas of the wagons began to flap crazily in the rising wind with the sound of damp battle flags.

Kate moved closer to the wagon the girls were riding in.

Quinn and Trace circled around to join her, concerned expressions on their faces.

"We're about to have a storm," Quinn said. "And look how those clouds are moving."

To the west, a dark cloud bank appeared to be playing shape games, swirling and moving strangely, compressing at places and thinning in others.

The now roaring wind, coming, it seemed from everywhere, drove stinging grit into Kate's face and tugged at her hat.

"Get the girls out of the wagon, Trace," she yelled above the relentless racket. "We'll put ourselves among rocks over there by the ridge. I think we may be in for a tornado and a big one, if I'm any judge."

"Where are Brock Davis and the Texans?" Trace said, shouting above the noise.

"They went to investigate some smoke rising to the southwest. I think he fears a prairie fire or bandits or both."

In the few moments it took the girls to

clamber out of the wagon, the weather had intensified and worsened. Roiling dark clouds covered much of the sky, and there was movement there, disturbance.

The tornado was the bastard child of a thunderstorm that had formed a hundred miles to the west. They could not know that, driven by a wind that reached almost two hundred and fifty miles an hour, its destructive path was a mile wide and forty long.

The twister's name was death . . . but Kate was still unaware.

"Brock said we should free the animals so they can fend for themselves," she said. "But we won't free them yet, not until we know —"

"Look there!" Quinn cried out, pointing.

A black, V-shaped column reached down from the clouds like an obsidian arrowhead.

They watched as the inky vortex slithered across the land like a rattlesnake waiting to strike, dancing first toward the wagons and then away.

"Where's it going?" Quinn yelled. "I can't tell where it's going."

The storm's track was impossible to anticipate, but it was moving fast and Kate had to take action.

"All of you, run for the rocks," Kate said.

Quinn looked hesitant.

"Now!" Kate screamed.

She and Trace moved to free the oxen from the wagons, but the funnel cloud veered toward them and then there was no time.

The oxen, terrified, stampeded and dragged the wagons with them.

Now the tornado, as fickle as a teenager at her first ball, made a fortunate turn away from them and roared across the flat with the sound of a thousand runaway locomotives.

A storm's hoarse bellow was a primitive, savage thing, as though the earth itself spewed its hatred.

Kate and the others cowered among the tumbled limestone rocks, but the vindictive wind found them and tore at hair, skin, and clothing.

Kate crawled close to Shannon and protected her with her own body. The child, scared stiff, clutched her ragdoll close and whimpered.

Kate reached out and closed her hand around Shannon's ankle, holding fast. "I've got you, sweetheart," Kate said, but her voice was carried away in the tornado's roar.

Later Quinn said that the funnel cloud came so close he saw a line of telegraph poles cartwheel past, then a tin rooster wind vane, and finally a red velvet sofa.

What happened next was so fast, and so horrible, that Kate never was able to fully put it together afterward.

Holding tight to Shannon's waist while keeping her own face as low and shielded against flying grit as possible, she felt her body grabbed by the wind and lifted six inches off the ground.

Then Shannon flailed her arm, her fingers grasping, as something blue flew from her hands and into the sky. The ruthless, roaring wind had taken her doll.

"Katie!" Shannon yelled.

She pushed against Kate, ready to run out into the open to save her doll.

Kate gripped the child even tighter. Her hat blew off and her red hair tossed around like flames from a log fire.

Shannon continued to yell, but exactly what she said Kate could not tell.

And then in a moment of nature's barbarity, Shannon's body catapulted into the air, jerked upward by a physical force stronger than any Kate had ever fought against.

She heard Shannon shriek and saw her youngest child, arms and legs spread wide, tumble through the air like a withered leaf in a fall storm.

Shannon's cries faded away into silence as

she caught up by the whirlwind and dragged inside the spinning column.

Kate tried to get up and go after her, but the wind was too strong.

She was thrown to the ground, pummeled unmercifully when she was down, and was forced to crawl back into the rocks, her teeth bared as the wind stole her breath.

Kate sank down into a space between the rocks and pushed her face into the dirt. From somewhere Trace yelled something, words she didn't understand. Ivy cried out and then fell silent.

The tornado, satisfied at the destruction it had wrought, spun its way to the east. Overhead the clouds thinned and the sky cleared and was blue again.

The roar of the wind gave way to an ominous calm. Crickets again made their small music in the warm grass.

Kate rose, pushed her hair out of her face, and her eyes reached out across the plain. Nothing moved.

Ivy came to her, trembling. "Mother, did Shannon . . ."

"I don't know," Kate said. "I saw the storm take her and then I saw no more."

Ivy's face was ashen.

"Oh God, Ma, is she . . ."

"I told you, I don't know," Kate said.

Then aware how sharp she'd sounded, she said, "We can hope for a miracle."

Trace clambered onto the tallest rock and studied the landscape.

"Ma, riders coming in."

Kate climbed up beside him and followed his pointing finger.

Moving toward them slowly was a man on horseback, a bundle in his arms.

Beside him rode one of the Texas guns. He led a horse that carried a man draped over the saddle.

Sunlight glinted on spurs and Kate realized that the dead man was the other guard.

As the riders drew closer, Trace yelled, "It's Brock Davis and I think he's carrying Shannon."

Kate scrambled down from the rocks so fast she fell. She picked herself up and, her skirts flying, ran toward the slowly advancing riders.

When Kate was close enough to shout, she said, "Is it Shannon?"

"It surely is, Mrs. Kerrigan," Davis said.

The little girl stirred, then squealed and held out her arms to Kate.

"Ma," Shannon said. "I've come home."

Davis drew rein and Kate took her daughter in her arms and hugged her close, covering her dirty little face with kisses.

"We found her, on the way back, Ma'am," Davis said. "She lay on the ground where the tornado dropped her as gentle as a feather on a snowbank, almost like it had laid her down to rest."

"The storm took her. Picked her up, and up, and . . ."

"Tornadoes are notional, Mrs. Kerrigan. They do unexpected things, blow down one house, spare another."

"God was looking out for her," Kate said.

"Yeah, I reckon so, though He's mighty notional His ownself," Davis said.

Only then, as Shannon clung to her, did Kate approach the dead man.

She looked up at the surviving Texan, a taciturn man with a long, hound dog face, and said, "What happened, Ben?"

"Lew got shot, Ma'am," he said.

Kate turned to Davis, seeking an explanation.

"Tell you about it later, Mrs. Kerrigan. The wagons are in good shape I see, but first we'd better round up the livestock. They're probably all scattered to hell and gone."

CHAPTER THIRTY-ONE

Brock Davis, Ben, and Trace rode in herding the oxen and horses.

"We've lost a horse and a couple of oxen, Ma'am," Davis told Kate. "But we can make do with what we have. It could've have been a lot worse."

Despite their joy over Shannon's safe return, the death of the man named Lew hung over the Kerrigans like a pall.

Davis decided that the dead man should be buried right away.

"We'll plant him before it gets too dark," he said. "I never did cotton to burying a man by lantern light."

Later they all stood around the grave as the day shaded into night and coyotes yipped in the distance.

"Does anyone wish to say anything?" Kate said. She held her worn Bible.

Lew lay gray and cold in the grave, but clean enough to meet his maker.

As is the way of the Irish women, Kate had washed the Texan's bloody body with her own hands.

"Ben, you were the closest thing to a friend Lew had," Davis said. "You want to say the words?"

The lanky Texan nodded.

Turning his hat in his hands, he looked down at the dead man.

"His name was Lew and he told me no other," he said. "He was a steady hand, fast on the draw and shoot, an' I reckon he's already drinking the devil's whiskey in hell. Amen."

A silence fell over the group that no one seemed overly anxious to fill.

Finally Kate said, "Thank you, Ben. That was very nice."

She bowed her head.

"We'll now say prayers for the immortal soul of Lew in the hope that he will enjoy life everlasting in the arms of our blessed Savior."

Ben nodded.

Then, emboldened by Kate's faint praise, he said, "He'll be sadly missed."

When the burial was done and the lonely grave left behind, Brock urged them to great caution in travel, because there were dangerous men about.

He revealed to Kate and Trace that the smoke he had investigated had been that of burning wagons from another, slightly larger wagon train than the Kerrigans' small one.

They had been destroyed by what had apparently been an attack of renegades, possibly Comancheros, though the notorious Rain Horse and his bandits could not be ruled out.

There had been bodies, mutilated, the women and girls misused before they died, Davis said.

The Kerrigans moved on and encountered no renegades, bandits, or Comancheros, and felt a lightening of spirits when finally they crossed into Texas.

Still miles upon miles to go to reach their specific destination, but they were closer to home.

Ivy drew closer to her mother and had become less critical and demanding.

Right after they'd crossed into Texas, she took her mother aside and said, "I heard what Mr. Brock told you and Trace about the wagon train that was attacked and burned," Ivy said. "And what I thought was, I'd rather die than have to suffer what the girls in the wagon train did."

"It won't come to that, Ivy," Kate said. "I

won't ever let it come to that."

The new Kerrigan ranch house near the Brazos headwaters, yet unfinished, took the breath away from the Kerrigans who were to live in it.

It was a far cry from the Gothic splendor of the Hagan mansion, but much better than anything they'd been used to.

"Joe, I wish you were here with me to see this together," Kate said.

Trace joined her. "I'm sure he sees it, Ma."

Kate smiled.

"I'm sure he does."

"Ma, when will you feel ready to tell us the reason Mr. Hagan seems so much like father?" Trace said.

Given all that had happened on the trail and their final arrival here on the Brazos, Kate could find no compelling reason not to speak, especially to the oldest of her children.

"I'll tell you now, Trace. But please tell none of the others. I will do that myself in my good time."

Trace nodded. "I'll keep your secret."

"Trace, the reason Cornelius Hagan so closely resembles your father is that they were sired by the same man, by your late grandfather who was constantly unfaithful to his wife. There is no need to throw a veil over it or pretend such things don't sometimes happen in this world. Your grandfather fathered two sons, one in wedlock, the other outside it, that latter one being our benefactor, Cornelius. Cornelius got his fortune through the father who raised him, named Hagan, but his physical traits, obviously, through the father who sired him."

"So I have a blood relation in Mr. Hagan."

"You do. All you children do."

"You didn't know, did you, when you first saw him, that he would be so much like Father. That was why you were so shocked."

"Yes. I looked at his face and saw the eyes of Joe Kerrigan. I'll admit it certainly took me by surprise. It was as if I was seeing him again, alive before me — almost as though your father had come back from beyond the grave. I could make no sense of it until I talked to Cornelius later, and he told me the truth about it all."

"Why did you not just tell us right away, when we wanted to know?"

"I was still trying to take it all in on my own. I didn't know what I should and should not say, and to whom."

"I'm glad to know now."

"Yes."

"It's going to be a good life here, Ma.

Quinn and me have talked it over with Ivy and Niall and Shannon and we're all going to pitch in and make this ranch a success, for the sake of us and for the memories of father and well, Ma, even for good old Ireland."

"Our own ranch, Trace. A future for us all."

"For us all."

Chapter Thirty-Two

For the Kerrigans' first days on the ranch, home was not the cabin currently being framed in by a crew of Hagan's hired workers, but a large barn about two hundred feet from the house.

Because the ranch was not yet operating, the barn was not in use except as a place for the builders to stable their horses and park their wagons.

The Kerrigan family moved into the empty loft area.

They bedded down each night on lumpy straw mattresses left there by the carpentry crew, which worked shifts, one group sleeping a few hours while the other labored. The workers were as starry-eyed over Kate as most men and readily agreed to give up their mattresses for use by the family.

Ivy said she felt much like a princess in one of the fairy tales Kate often told the girls as bedtime stories, unable to nod off because the straw was "poking her like that pea."

But she stopped complaining after Trace pointed out that the straw beds were "a lot cleaner than the one I slept on when I was running from the law back in Nashville, and there's no vermin here, either."

Some of the more thoughtful carpenters took kindness a step further and enclosed some rough rooms in the loft to allow for a degree of privacy and protection from the cool night winds that frequently lanced between the timber slats.

Kate discovered that a ventilation window in the wall of the barn's loft provided a good view of the house's progress as well as the Texas brush flats that seemed to stretch forever.

She charmed one of the carpenters into making her a chair from some of the lumber scrap and enjoyed sitting with her coffee in the mornings, looking out on what she was sure would be part of her own ranch one day.

She was enjoying that view one waning afternoon when she caught sight of Ivy and Niall darting out into the plains, throwing back and forth a ball Ivy had crafted from an old sock she'd stuffed with one thing or another.

She smiled, watching her twins enjoying their sport, but a chill ran through her veins when she glanced up beyond them and saw, on top of a low rise, several horsemen.

At first Kate thought the riders were assessing the progress of the cabin, but a closer look persuaded her the men were actually watching her twins at play. Worried now, she wondered what manner of men these were and why they were there.

Then she saw one of the riders, a bearded, uncurried man with a greasy mane of hair falling to his shoulders, walking his horse down the low rise in the direction of the children.

Fear mixed with concern, Kate turned away from her window and headed to the ladder leading down from the loft to the barn floor. She all but leaped the last half of the distance, and grabbed the Henry that stood against the frame of the door as she went out.

Rifle in hand, she ran hard toward the house.

One of the workmen saw her.

"Hey, Mrs. Kerrigan, what's wrong?" he yelled.

Wordlessly Kate pointed violently in the general direction of her twins and the horsemen beyond them.

As she drew close enough for her children to notice her, they in fact did not do so, because the burly, bearded rider was not twelve feet away from Ivy.

The little girl was looking bravely up at him, and Kate recognized Ivy's posture as that she presented when she was afraid.

Something the man was saying to her, or maybe merely the way he looked at her, scared the girl.

Kate eyed the other horsemen and was pleased to see they had not moved from the rise. Only the big man that loomed over Ivy had moved.

"Hey you!" Kate called. "Get the hell away from my daughter."

She held the Henry at her waist, the muzzle pointed at the big intruder.

Her voice startled Niall, who was nearest her, and made Ivy turn her head fast to look.

The man on the horse looked her way, too, heavy brows hanging low over his eyes like gigantic black caterpillars.

"You talking to me, lady?"

"Yes, I'm talking to you. Is there anyone else near my daughter?"

His eyes did an up-and-down sweep of Kate, giving her an appraisal she was accustomed to receiving from all sorts of men.

"So this is your daughter, is she? Well,

Ma'am, I can see where the sweet little lady gets her fine looks. Same as me, I got mine from my mama's side of the family."

"Who are you?"

"Name's Bodine, Ma'am. Bill Bodine at your service. And let me take a guess here. You're the Kerrigan woman who everybody says is building that there ranch house."

"What is your concern with me or my family, Bodine? State your intentions."

"Well, Ma'am, you're a right tart-tongued woman, that I'll say. All I was doing, Ma'am, was asking your little miss if she could point me to the foreman so I could ask about maybe finding a little work here."

"It would seem to me that most men looking for work wouldn't assume that a little girl playing ball with her brother would be a likely place to start inquiring."

"Just fond of children, I am. Me and my friends back there, we're all fond of the young'uns." He yelled. "Ain't that right, boys?"

A couple of faint grunts were all the response received.

Kate knew just what Bodine was doing in calling back to them: he was reminding her that he was not alone, and that there was but one of her, several of them.

"Mrs. Kerrigan, can I ask you why you're

hauling that Henry around?"

"You can ask, and I'm glad to answer. I am carrying this rifle because, had you laid a hand on my little girl, I was going to use it to put a bullet in your head."

"Damn it all, woman! Oh, sorry about the cuss in front of tender little ears. But I got to say, Ma'am, that's might mean-hearted of you, talking about killing a man. Why're you so angry, ma'am?"

"I nearly lost a daughter recently and since then I've become awfully fierce when it comes to protecting my children. When I see a stranger approach my child for no good reason, one like you who has the look of the outlaw about him, I grab this here Henry."

"I ain't hurt your girl, Ma'am. Never would do such a thing. Like I said, I love the young'uns." Then louder, "Yes, I love them a lot, and the ladies, too."

Laughter rippled through the riders on the ridge and angered Kate so greatly she would gladly have triggered the Henry and shot it out with them right then and there.

Hearing someone approaching from behind her, she turned and was relieved to see it was Brock Davis.

He was armed with a pair of Colts.

Brock glared at the riders. "Where's your

friend Rain Horse?"

The riders glanced at one another, and Bodine kneed his horse closer.

Davis, almost casually, as though he didn't really mean to do it, pointed the Colts in the direction of Bodine's big belly.

"Damned unfriendly folks around here," Bodine said.

"I asked you where Rain Horse is."

"Not here, that's where he is," Bodine said. "Last I seen him he was talking about going to be with his kept woman. She's got a cabin up in the Nations that he likes to go to. If I was a betting man, I'd bet that's where he is."

"You're Bill Bodine."

"I am indeed, sir. And pray, who are you?"

"My name is Brock Davis. And I'm going to ask you to get down off that horse, Bodine. I know some of your history, and I think it's time to deal with it."

"You some kind of lawman, Davis?"

"Not a bit of it. Just got no use for them who hurt innocent folk for their own entertainment."

Bodine looked at Kate. "You may want to take these children away. I think it's about to get ugly around here."

Kate said, "Can we handle this many?"

"She makes a good point there, Mr. Davis," Bodine said. "If'n I was you I'd holster them Colts and find someplace to disappear to. You've put me in a bad mood."

"No matter what happens, Bodine," Kate said. "You get my first bullet."

"But not today, lady. I like to bide my time, like."

Bodine glared at Davis.

"I'm riding away. You'll have to shoot me in the back, and you just don't look the type, if you know what I mean."

"Don't put your faith in how I look, Bodine," Davis said.

The big man swung his horse around and Kate and Davis waited until he and his companions rode away.

When the renegades were out of sight, Kate said, "Come children, let's get away from here. This is no company for us to be keeping. Will you come with us, Brock?"

"I have a bad feeling about that bunch," Davis said.

"And so have I," Kate said.

"We ain't seen the last of them."

"That's why I'm sleeping tonight with my Henry beside me," Kate said.

CHAPTER THIRTY-THREE

In the night, the frame of the rising cabin was like the skeleton of a giant animal slain on the Texas flats.

So it seemed to young Niall Kerrigan as he walked back toward the barn from the rough outhouse that served for the only privy facilities on the construction site. Built for the use of the house builders, it now also served the barn-dwelling Kerrigans, and Niall despised having to make the long walk in the night just to answer a call of nature. It was troublesome, and the moon shadows cast by the cabin's frame were eerie to a nine-year-old boy. Who would soon be ten, he reminded himself. His and Ivy's shared birthday was coming up in just over a week. They would no longer be little children whose age could be shown in a single digit. For the rest of their lives, unless they lived very long indeed, they would have two-digit ages. Like grown-ups.

It made Niall grin when he thought about the fact they resided in a barn now, since the house wasn't far enough along for use. Like being a cow, or a horse. Kind of funny.

No cow or horse, though, snored the way Mr. Brock did, or so Niall figured. The wagon master turned general family aide and protector could saw logs with the best of them. Not tonight, though. Mr. Brock was not present, but gone again to the tiny settlement of Cornwall, on down the road about a mile and a quarter, to spend the night in the room up above the little saloon that was the heart, and most of the substance, of the tiny crossroads community. Niall had wondered aloud to Trace and Quinn if maybe Mr. Brock did that because the bed there was more comfortable than the straw ticks on which everybody slept in the barn loft.

They'd laughed at him, and Trace had said there was a lot more to it than that. "Brock's found him a woman there," Trace had said. "The easy-to-find kind, who'll let you be her fella if you'll pay her for it." Then he and Quinn had laughed and nudged one another as if they thought they were worldly fellows, much more manly than Niall.

Ha! Niall could have told them he understood more things than his big brothers realized. He knew how things worked, why tomcats came bawling around writhing cats in the darkness at certain times, and why bulls jumped up on the backs of cows in that way that had always made Ivy laugh and point and tell everyone to "look — the cows are dancing."

Stupid Ivy. Now *there* was a child, even though she and Niall were exactly the same age. Girls just didn't understand things the way boys did. They were naïve and innocent and silly that way. Even though Ivy had emerged from the womb first, he'd always seen himself as a little older than his twin sister.

Niall wasn't sure that Ivy had even grasped why that repellent man with the big beard had acted so strangely around her earlier in the day. She'd known there was something off and odd and probably dangerous about him, but he doubted she had a clue about what was behind it. Niall knew. The man was the sort that Quinn always called a "dirty fellow." One who spent too much time thinking about women and girls and the things that could be done with them, and to them — girls way too young to be thought about that way, in the bearded man's case. And that man, the one called Bodine, he probably did more than just think about them, Niall supposed.

The man had frightened him, and made him shudder in a deep-inside kind of way. There'd been something wicked and scary about him, and those other men who had been with him. Ivy had felt it, too, Niall thought — felt it but not understood just what it was. She'd refused to talk to Niall about it afterward, or let him talk to her.

Niall eyed the skeleton of the house again as he passed before it, and thought how big it seemed. Things got big like that, he supposed, when rich men were behind them.

The Kerrigans had always lived a cramped life, though their flat in Nashville hadn't been nearly as crowded as their mother's childhood dwelling in the Five Points of New York had been, to hear her tell it. She'd grown up with her parents, herself, and her younger sister all sharing a two-room space. Not big rooms, either. But they had had it good, compared to some.

His ma had told him there were tenements in the Five Points where fifteen or twenty people might sleep on the same floor in a single room, lying on rags and such because there were no real beds. Dirty, noise-making, muttering, snoring, wind-breaking people who flopped about like fish on dry land, able to sleep, usually, only because they were so drunk.

The Five Points stories Kate told her children had made the place seem like hell on earth to Niall, who had a natural aversion to being cramped up and compressed. His mother had told him that came from having been a twin, being crowded even in the womb. Made sense to Niall. Ivy had the same dislike of small spaces that he did.

Niall studied the dark shell of the new house. Being crowded wouldn't be a problem here. There would be big rooms, many windows, and all he had to do if he ever felt cramped was throw the door open and head outside onto the plains.

Ma said Mr. Hagan, who did all things big, had designed this house himself, and he'd made sure their family would have a comfortable space to move around in. God bless Mr. Hagan for that, Niall thought. For that and so many other things.

"When I grow up," Niall whispered to himself in the moonlight, "I'm going to be a rich man, too." It was a sensible ambition, as he figured it. If everybody were rich, nobody would have to do without food, or shelter, or decent clothes for their backs or shoes for their feet. Yep, rich was the way to go.

He looked up at the cabin's shell a little

longer, wondering which room he'd sleep in and he imagined his ma sitting by the fire at night with her sewing in this wonderful new place — and his thoughts made the scary-looking house skeleton not seem scary anymore. The Kerrigan home would be a warm and happy place, secure and roomy. Oh, it was going to be fun.

Niall turned to go back to the barn and get a little more sleep before the morning arrived. He'd taken only five steps when he stopped in his tracks.

He squinted hard, watching what was unfolding before him, and wondering if he was seeing what he thought he was. A cold wave of horror dashed over him like icy water, and he stayed frozen in place, hoping that by being still, he would go unnoticed.

Apparently it worked, because a few moments later they were gone and the barn was just a big and dark old barn again. Catching breath Niall had been holding without even realizing it, the boy raced toward the barn and up the ladder, and went straight to the makeshift room where his mother slept.

"Wake up, Mama! You got to wake up now!"

Kate Kerrigan raised up from her straw mattress on the floor, her hair a jumble from sleep. "Niall? What's wrong, honey?"

"They got her, Mama. They got Ivy. They took her away, just now! I was coming back from the outhouse and I saw it! They carried her away, Mama! And . . . and I just stood there because I was too afraid to move." He began to cry.

Kate didn't even have to ask. Her mind filled with the image of that big, foul, bearded man, and the human trash that sat their horses behind him. They hadn't come to the work site in hope of finding work. They hadn't even approached the work crew to ask for it. They'd come to look over the pickings at the picnic — to make their selection for later.

Later had come. They had come back.

They had Ivy.

Quinn's feet slammed the dirt, sending up clouds of dust that caught the moonlight, and his chest heaved and side hurt. Still a quarter mile to go. He strained and pushed himself, wondering if that stitch in his side, worsening with every step, was anything that could actually do him harm. Probably not, but God, it hurt!

Why had his mother sent him for this task, he wondered. Wouldn't it have been better for lightweight, fleet little Niall to be sent to run to get Brock rather than dumpy old Quinn? Quinn had been out of breath before he'd made it half a mile. He'd pushed himself on anyway, hard, lungs heaving and burning. He was doing this for Ivy, and he'd run himself to death if he had to.

Realizing he'd slowed more than he should, he stopped for a moment, let his lungs heave some air, and then started running again. He prayed hard for strength, and told God that after this he'd work on making himself stronger and faster in case he was ever called upon to do something like this again. He hoped to high heaven that would never happen.

Keeping his eyes fixed ahead, looking for the humble outline of Cornwall, Texas, against the flatlands and dark blur of a horizon, Quinn ran and ran and ran some more, ignoring pain and straining lungs. There! There it was, just coming into the dimmest of views. He saw the big stable, the false-fronted general store, the little shoebox of a church house built by a little gaggle of Methodists — and the saloon. That, plus a couple of thrown-together houses and outbuildings, comprised all there was to see in Cornwall, Texas.

With his destination now in view, Quinn

ran even harder, and he quickly reached the front door. He knew it would be unlocked. Curly Small never closed his saloon, though at night he cranked down the lamp that lit the place and retired to sleep on his lonely cot in the back room. But Curly slept with an ear always open for the jangle of the bell that told him when somebody had come in the front door. A man of business had to be ready to attend at any hour.

Quinn slammed through and pounded across the floor of lumber that was varnished only with the residue of a hundred spilled drinks and a thousand splatters of tobacco-infused spittle.

He was vaguely aware of Curly appearing in the doorway to the back room just as Quinn hit the base of the staircase. Curly was but a ghost in dirty long underwear, and there was no time to talk to him and explain.

Quinn took the stairs two at a time, and despite his panic, proud of himself that he had pulled off the feat of running a mile and a quarter, yet could still bound up a staircase.

From behind the closed door at the end of the short hallway, he heard the now-familiar rumble of Brock's distinctive snoring. Whatever else might have gone on behind that door earlier in the evening, it was down to simple sleeping now.

Quinn hammered the door with fist and forearm. "Mr. Brock! Wake up, Mr. Brock! It's Quinn!" He was gasping so hard it was difficult to get out the words.

A muffled female voice, cursing and murmuring. The squeak of a bed upon which people were sitting up abruptly. The replacement of Brock's snores with grunts and guttural exclamations of, "What the hell . . ."

The door opened and a disheveled, scantily clad woman glared out at him, her mouth hanging open, breath tainted with the stink from her habit of smoking hand-rolled quirlies and drinking Curly's stale beer, and never cleaning her yellowed teeth. "Who are you, you little shit?"

Quinn had no time for this. He rudely shoved the woman aside and burst into the room. Brock, shirtless, was sitting up on the bed, looking sleep-drunk and puzzled.

"Quinn, what are you —"

"You got to come, sir. Now! They've taken Ivy away. A whole bunch of 'em! They came today and watched her, then they came back in the night and took her."

"Who? Wha—"

"I think it's the same bad men who come down from up in the Nations — the ones who ride with that Indian called Rain Horse. Except he wasn't with them today, when they came, I don't think. There was a big man, with a beard, name of Bodine."

The prostitute put her fingertips to the base of her throat and gasped. "Oh, God! Bill Bodine! If he's took some woman, it's going to be hell for her. I know the son of a . . . I know what he likes."

Brock, dressing now, said, "Did you say it was Ivy they took?"

"Yes, sir. Niall saw them carry her away."

Brock looked at his whore. "They've not taken away a woman, Belle. Ivy is a little girl. Nine, maybe ten years old."

The prostitute, who had surely lost most of her feminine sympathies and tenderness long ago, had tears on her face. A little girl, in the hands of a man who (perhaps she knew from personal experience) was a sadist and monster. And the men with him, no better. And Rain Horse, should he enter the picture, worst of all.

"Come on, Quinn," Brock said, strapping on his Remington-laden gun belt, which had been hanging on a hat tree in the corner. "There's no time to waste."

CHAPTER THIRTY-FOUR

By the time Davis's horse galloped to a halt at the Kerrigan house construction site, Quinn riding double behind Brock, the first streaks of dawn were lighting the sky. They found Niall sitting tensely on the ground against the front wall of the barn, holding tight to a hatchet that was his favorite possession, and little more, really, than a toy.

"Where are they, boy?" Brock asked.

Niall, wordless and numb, pointed north, out across the Texas flatlands, miles beyond which lay the southern border of the Indian Nations.

"Did Kate go?"

"Yes."

"Is she armed?"

"She has her rifle."

Brock had a hopeless manner about him that scared Quinn. He didn't have to be told that the situation was dire, but Brock's stance and tension intensified the awareness.

"A woman, against a gang of devils like that! That's a mother for you, boys. That's what you call a mother taking on the devil himself if it's for the sake of her child." He rubbed his face. "Where's Trace? Did he go with your mother?"

"No, he saddled up early and left. He said he'd find Ivy and kill the men who took her."

"I hope to hell Trace doesn't go up against Rain Horse and his men," Davis said. "He won't walk away from it."

"We'd best go, Mr. Brock," Quinn said.

"You're staying here, with Niall," Brock said.

"I got to go with you, sir. It's my sister!"

"It is, and if it can be done, I'll bring her back to you." He put himself between Niall and Quinn, his back to Niall.

"Quinn," he said quietly, "you have a terrified little brother there. You need to be here to keep guard over him."

Quinn couldn't guess what Niall would need guarding against when it was Ivy who was in trouble, but this was no time for debating. "Yes, sir."

Brock went to his saddlebags and from one of them produced a small Colt revolver.

He handed it to Quinn. "It's already loaded," he said. "Just in case, you know."

Seconds later, Brock was riding away, going the way Niall had pointed.

Niall looked at the pistol in his brother's hand. "If that man with the beard came back here right now, I'd shoot him with the pistol. Right through the heart."

"No, you wouldn't," Quinn said.

"Would so!"

Quinn shook his head. "You wouldn't have the chance. I'd be using it myself, shooting him right in the face."

Niall nodded. "That would be good." He looked toward the shell of the house. No workers would be there that day, it being Sunday. "Quinn, will they hurt Ivy?"

Quinn could not lie. "They might, Niall. They might."

"Take a look at that there, Bill," said the hairless piece of human vermin known as Steel Chandler. "What do you reckon that is?"

"It's a wagon of some kind, best I can tell," Bodine said. Like Steel, he was on horseback. Nestled in front of him, hands tied to the saddle horn, was Ivy Kerrigan, a trembling and very small human form he held back tightly against him with his left arm, his massive beard hanging down over her left shoulder, scratching against her tear-stained face.

"Not the usual kind of wagon you see in these parts," Steel observed. He looked over at Ivy, caught her eye, and winked. "Hey, little thing, you looking forward to playing with me and nice Mr. Bodine here? Huh? You looking forward to that?"

He'd asked that same question at least five times already, and Ivy had only the vaguest and most disturbing idea of what he was hinting at. The games she liked were the ones like she'd played earlier in the day, tossing that ball back and forth with her brother. She doubted the bald man was talking about anything like that. All she knew was that she wanted to play no games at all with these men. They were ugly, mean, bad. They even *smelled* bad.

Steel, watching and listening, chuckled evilly. "Rain Horse is going to like that one, like her a lot!" he said, grinning at her.

"Not till *I'm* through with her, and that may take a while," said Bodine, giving Ivy a hug.

Steel got down from his saddle and walked a few feet away, looking at the wagon that had drawn his attention. It was parked out on the flats, a little smoke rising from the round chimney pipe that extended from its top.

No canvas-topped wagon this one. It was fully enclosed with something like a little house built onto its long, broad bed.

Painted so it even *looked* like a house, with colorful windows and doors and porch columns.

Steel had no way of knowing he was seeing a painted version in miniature of the Hagan mansion up in Kansas, because this strange, ornate wagon, pulled by huge and powerful oxen under the control of a black-skinned driver who was himself nearly as huge and powerful as the oxen he drove, belonged to the vastly wealthy Cornelius Hagan, who at the moment was outside the wagon, unseen by Steel because the huge moving house blocked him from view.

Hagan was having his first urination of the day, admiring his view of the plains as the morning brightened over them.

Hagan was on his way south, following the way taken by his recent guests, Kate Kerrigan and children. They'd not been gone from his estate for two days before he'd started thinking about following them, seeing for himself that all was going according to his direction and the house construction was on schedule, and up to quality.

In truth, he was going because he was finding it miserable to be away from Kate, after having grown used to having her around.

No finer woman had he ever known, none he had more wish to be near. He'd not foreseen falling in love when he'd decided to give aid to his late half-brother's widow and her brood.

It had happened, though.

His driver, Farley, who knew him maybe better than anyone else, had detected it quickly. Hagan had taken a little longer to recognize the truth and admit it, even to himself.

His newly blossoming love inspired Hagan to hurry completion of his new "Rolling Mansion" vehicle, the excellent wagon, as ornate as a tycoon's personal railroad car, that he might have allowed the Kerrigans to use for their Texas journey had it been finished.

So he had put his wagon builders to constructing traditional wagons for the journeying family, and had reserved "Rolling Mansion" for himself.

Hagan had hurried his wagon makers mercilessly, and set out southward the day after the wagon was declared finished.

Not far now.

They should reach the vicinity of the small town of Cornwall and the nearby Kerrigan cabin this very day.

Hagan was so excited he could hardly restrain himself from dancing. His only qualm about this venture was that he wasn't sure that Brock Davis wasn't as interested in Kate as he was.

It was worry over Brock that had provided a handy pretext to launch the journey of pursuit, and it didn't matter much, anyway. Kate was the kind of woman that almost every man fell for upon meeting her.

Farley was the designated cook as well as the driver, and had a fire going already, bacon sizzling in a heavy iron skillet and biscuits baking in a Dutch oven.

The smell was intolerably good, and Hagan was starved.

He paced around restlessly, eager to get to his breakfast.

Hagan walked past the front of the wagon and glanced to his left.

To his surprise, he saw horsemen, five or six of them, at a standstill off to the east. They were just far away enough that he couldn't make out much about them, though the closest of them, who was down off his horse and facing Hagan's way was as bald as an egg.

Still mounted was a huge, burly man with a flowing beard and some sort of sack, or bedroll, or something, clutched in front of him on the saddle.

Hagan squinted, trying to make out just what it was, and then he remembered the field glasses that Farley kept beneath his seat whenever he was on driving duty.

Something kept drawing Hagan's eye back to the big man and the unidentified thing he clutched before him.

Squinting even harder, Hagan gasped suddenly, and rushed to fetch Farley's field glasses.

From the driver's platform that was Farley's domain, Hagan looked toward the horsemen through the field glasses. The bald man was getting into his saddle again. He swept the glass to the right a little bit, and what he saw filled him with horror and disbelief.

It was as it had seemed — the thing in front of the big man was not a thing at all, but was a small child. A girl. And as Hagan adjusted the focus, he saw her face.

God in heaven —

It was Ivy Kerrigan.

CHAPTER THIRTY-FIVE

Kate Kerrigan and Brock Davis had searched all night and had seen nothing of Ivy and her captors.

Trace was also out there somewhere and Kate wondered if her son had better luck.

Then as a scarlet dawn painted the sky, Davis drew rein and Kate did the same.

His face drawn and tired, as she knew hers must be, Davis straightened in the saddle and worked knots out of his shoulders.

Finally he said, "Kate, we're splitting up to cover more ground. There's a settlement about an hour to the to west called Cornwall. It's just possible Rain Horse and his boys have taken Ivy there."

"Possible but not likely," Kate said.

She was all used up and her horse was tired.

Hope was fading in her, but she was determined not to give up the chase.

"We must check it out," Davis said. "I'll

go if you'd rather scout to the south again."

Kate shook her head.

"No, I'll go."

"How are you holding up?" Davis said.

"Not well. You?"

"Fine," Davis said. "Just fine."

But his exhausted face gave the lie to that answer.

Kate nodded.

"Then let's ride, Brock. I'll see you back at the cabin when . . ."

"When this is over and Ivy is safe."

"Yes," Kate said. "When this is over."

"Farley!" Hagan called. "Come here and take a look, and tell me I'm wrong — because this time I want to be wrong. Is that Ivy Kerrigan in the saddle with that man over there? You remember her? The little daughter of Kate Kerrigan with a brother the same age?"

A far-sighted man, Farley took the field glasses and looked for himself.

Hagan saw the man's jaw set into hard iron. He lowered the field glasses and looked at his boss.

"Well?" Hagan said. "Tell me man, is it her or not?"

"You ain't wrong, boss. No sir. That's her, that's Miss Ivy, and I don't think that man's supposed to have her like that."

Farley looked again and knew he might be studying the face of a man he was soon to kill.

It was obvious that Ivy was not where she was willingly, nor happy to be undergoing such a crude pawing by a bear of a man.

Though he'd sometimes found the child to be a bit of a grouch, Farley had developed a protective affection for Ivy during the time she had been at the Hagan house.

The girl had often helped him attend to the huge oxen, the very ones now yoked to the wagon.

"We're going to have to forget breakfast for now, good as it smells," Hagan said.

"I know, boss, I know. You got your shotgun in the back?"

"I do."

"You'd best fetch it. We may be facing a gun trouble this morning."

With that, the six-foot-six Farley reached into the storage compartment beneath him, replaced the field glasses, and in its place drew out a sawed-off shotgun, and a gun belt and holstered Navy Colt.

He buckled the belt around his lean waist as Hagan got back into the wagon.

Then Farley did an odd thing.

He jumped from the wagon, fetched the

Dutch oven, and clambered back up to his perch with it.

He sat the oven at his feet and got the wagon rolling, turning it toward the horsemen to the east.

Steel Chandler looked past the long, westward-stretching shadows he and his companions cast in the rising sun, and watched the suddenly changing situation out on the plains.

"Take a look, Bodine! They're a-coming our way with some kind of huge wagon."

"What the hell you reckon?" Bodine said.

He leaned down and gave Ivy a little kiss on the face with his hairy lips.

He'd caught a distant whiff of frying bacon a few minutes earlier, and it had made him drool, so his whiskers were wet where he kissed Ivy. It sickened her and she leaned to one side and dry heaved. Her empty stomach had nothing to give up, but it tried hard.

One of the horsemen behind Bodine saw this and laughed.

This was a man Bodine despised above all his usual cohorts, a weasel with a high-pitched, cackling laugh that grated in Bodine's ears and was always loudest with the joke was at Bodine's expense.

"Wilton, that's the last from you," Bodine said.

He reached to his holster, drew his Colt and shot Wilton through the heart.

Wilton's high-pitched laugh changed to an equally high-pitched yelp, and he slumped leftward, his head landing on the lap of the rider beside him.

The man frowned, made a sound of disgust, and pushed Wilton away.

Wilton dropped between the horses, his left foot remaining in its stirrup. The horse, startled by Wilton's fall, stepped to the right, and then walked away from the others, dragging Wilton by the leg.

"Laugh now, Wilton!" Bodine said, and then he delivered a scornful imitation of Wilton's cackle.

Farley drove up to the group and halted. The horsemen wheeled sufficiently to face him.

"Pretty morning, gentlemen," Farley said in his best imitation of a British accent, something he pulled off quite well, and which he'd used several times in the past to make Ivy laugh.

Only at that moment, hearing it, did Ivy realize who had just arrived.

"Mr. Farley!" she declared, lurching upward and bumping the top of her head against Bodine's bearded chin. It caused him to clamp his mouth shut and bite his tongue.

He swore foully at Ivy, grabbed her by the face and twisted her head to look up at him, and cursed her again.

With his bitten tongue tasting its own blood, Bodine shoved Ivy off the horse. She squealed and fell hard on the ground, the wind knocked out of her lungs.

Farley sighed. "Bad mistake, sir," he said. "I know that young lady and now I've got to kill you."

He retained the fake British accent.

Bodine glared at him. "You hear that, boys?" he said to his companions. "Got us one of them *fancy* colored boys here, talking all *special*! Says he's going to *kill* me! I don't think so."

Bodine lifted his revolver and leveled it at Farley.

Down the length of its barrel he saw Farley reach under the wagon seat and come up with a shotgun.

Bodine, unnerved by the scattergun, fired too quickly and missed.

The shotgun in the black man's hands roared. Bodine's big belly exploded as the buckshot hit and he screamed.

He stared at the blood and guts oozing

319

from him then at the man who'd killed him.

"Many apologies, my good fellow," said Farley. "As I mentioned, I know the young lady."

CHAPTER THIRTY-SIX

Stunned by the violence that had descended on them, the men with Bodine did not react right away.

The first to break out of his shock was Steel.

He pulled the machete from the scabbard hanging on his saddle and charged at Farley.

A .44 bullet from Kate Kerrigan's Henry crashed into the side of Steel's head.

With the last of his draining strength, the man threw the machete at Farley.

The black man dodged the spinning blade easily and Steel died with a look of bitter disappointment on his face.

The remaining riders went for their guns, their entire focus on the grinning black man.

Farley fired, missed, and threw down his shotgun.

He skinned his Colt.

Farley fired and a man and horse went down.

A shot grazed his shoulder and drew blood.

Now it was close work and Farley was not known for his skill with a revolver.

He was embroiled in a gunfight he could not win.

But then Kate Kerrigan, like an avenging angel, was among them.

Her horse at the gallop, she leaned away from Bodine's men and fired from the hip.

She killed a man, then, as the two others fought to regain control of their spooked horses, fired again. A clean miss.

But now both Farley and Hagan were back in the fight.

Hagan's shotgun blasted a man's arm off below the elbow and Farley scored a chest hit on the second.

And then it was all over.

Kate trotted back to a scene of carnage and swung out of the saddle.

She ran to Ivy, dropped on one knee, and held her close.

Only one horseman remained, a small man with the face of a vicious ape.

"I'm out of it," he said. "None of this was my doing."

"Wait here, Ivy," Kate said, getting to her feet.

"But Ma . . ."

"Wait here. Don't move."

Kate racked a round into the Henry's chamber.

Farley gave the little man a fake look of sympathy, dropped the British inflections, and said, "Get off the hoss and come here, friend."

Farley reached down and opened the Dutch oven. He selected a biscuit and handed it to the small man.

"Enjoy, Rain Horse,"

The bandit leader sniffed the biscuit.

"Did your hands make this, black man?" he said.

"Sure did," Farley said.

Rain Horse threw it away.

He looked at Hagan.

"I have surrendered," he said.

"Not to me you didn't," Kate said.

The bandit turned his head slowly in Kate's direction.

"I want you," he said.

"Too bad," Kate said.

Her .44 bullets tore great holes in the little man's body and coldly she watched him drop dead to the ground.

"No one harms mine," she said, gunsmoke curling around her.

Farley climbed down from the wagon and

hugged the sobbing Ivy close.

The girl clung to him, her head on his shoulder. Her slender body shuddered, as the terrible events of the morning caught up to her.

"It's all right, honey child," Farley said. "I'm here, and everything is all right. They're gone now."

"Thank you, Farley," she said. "Thank you."

"Why, tally ho and all that," he said, putting on again the false accent that so amused her. "Would you fancy a biscuit, milady?"

"Yes," she said. "I'd love one."

Ivy was eating her second biscuit when Trace Kerrigan arrived.

He rode in slowly, staring at the dead men scattered on the prairie grass.

Ivy seemed alive and well, eating a biscuit, beside someone who should not be here at all, Hagan's employee, Farley. And not far away, Hagan himself.

One big, bearded man lay a little away from the others. Trace was standing over him, looking down.

"Ma," Trace said. "This one's still alive."

Bodine's chest was moving a little, lungs partially visible, inflating and shakily deflating, in the great bloody cavity where his belly had been.

Kate walked over and looked down at the fleshy, pallid face of a dying man. Ivy joined her, slipping her hand into her mother's. The sight of Bodine's ruined form was nothing a little girl should experience, but Ivy was fast growing adept at dealing with things a child had no business experiencing.

"His name is Bill Bodine," Ivy said. "He was the one who grabbed me and kept me with him. He was going to do . . . things to me. I don't know exactly what, but I know it was going to be bad."

Bodine's eyes fluttered open and he looked up at Ivy, then at her mother. "Please," he managed to whisper to Kate. "I don't . . . want to die . . . help me, please. I'm not ready to die! Not ready . . ."

Kate nodded.

"No, I'm quite sure you're not."

Trace pulled his Colt from his waistband, cocked it, and aimed it at Bodine's forehead.

"You're a bad man, Bodine," he said. "Some men just don't deserve to live."

The sound of Trace's shot brought it all to an end.

They returned to the wagon and the process of putting the pieces together began.

Brock Davis met them on the trail home, a man almost completely in the dark as to what had and was happening.

He was greeted warmly, and was fully puzzled to see Hagan and Farley there.

"What brings you, Brock?" Farley asked. "You're running a little late, as usual."

Brock tried to find words, and at first could only shrug.

"I smelled biscuits," he said at last.

"You're in luck, my good man," Farley said, and he reached for the Dutch oven.

CHAPTER THIRTY-SEVEN

Kate Kerrigan finished her story and Hiram Street was silent for a while, then said, "And then what happened, Ma'am?"

Kate smiled and rose to her feet.

"Hiram, that's a story for another time," she said.

The young cowboy stood, as manners demanded.

"Will you tell it to me some time, boss?" he said. "I mean, everything that happened afterward?"

"Some time, Hiram. Now this old lady is heading for bed and you to the bunkhouse."

Street glanced out the parlor window.

"Look at the sky, Ma'am. Ain't it purty?"

The new aborning day was coming in clean, under ribbons of scarlet and jade cloud. Over by the barn a little calico cat yawned and stretched then went about her business.

"Miz Kerrigan," Street said, "I'm a man

who never took a serious view of things, but I reckon maybe I'll change. You went through much."

"Hiram, what I told you was only the start," Kate said.

She beckoned the cowboy to the window.

"You see the rock ridge to the north, by the wild oak?"

Street nodded.

"There's a grave up there, ain't there, Ma'am?"

"Yes," Kate said. "It doesn't have a marker because I wanted it that way."

"Who lies there?" Street said.

"A man, a terrible man that nowadays the people who write stories call a gunfighter. His name was Jack Hickam and he was fast, lightning fast on the draw and shoot. He'd killed eighteen men, or so they said."

"How did he end up there on the ridge?" the cowboy said.

"He was killed on the ridge in the summer of 1878 and we buried him right where he fell. In the rain. Then I spat on his grave."

"You done for him, boss?"

Kate smiled and said, "As I told you, Hiram, that's a story for another day."

After the cowboy left, Kate stepped out of the house, stood on the porch and leaned a shoulder on a soaring white column, one of four that fronted the Kerrigan mansion.

In the distance, the bunkhouse cook carried an armload of firewood to the kitchen. Kate waved and the man grinned and waved back.

She gazed out at her land where her cattle grazed.

Wild, proud and magnificent, it was a land Kate had never tamed.

But she had learned to live with it and adapt herself to its ways.

Trace and Quinn would ride in soon, eager for coffee and breakfast.

Kate yawned, fatigue finally catching up to her.

She went back inside, changed her mind about seeking her bed and changed into a morning dress.

When her sons arrived, she had another story to tell.

J. A. JOHNSTONE
ON WILLIAM W. JOHNSTONE
"WHEN THE TRUTH BECOMES LEGEND"

William W. Johnstone was born in southern Missouri, the youngest of four children. He was raised with strong moral and family values by his minister father, and tutored by his schoolteacher mother. Despite this, he quit school at age fifteen.

"I have the highest respect for education," he says, "but such is the folly of youth, and wanting to see the world beyond the four walls and the blackboard."

True to this vow, Bill attempted to enlist in the French Foreign Legion ("I saw Gary Cooper in *Beau Geste* when I was a kid and I thought the French Foreign Legion would be fun") but was rejected, thankfully, for being underage. Instead, he joined a traveling carnival and did all kinds of odd jobs. It was listening to the veteran carny folk, some of whom had been on the circuit since the late 1800s, telling amazing tales about their experiences, which planted the storytelling seed in Bill's imagination.

"They were mostly honest people, despite the bad reputation traveling carny shows had back then," Bill remembers. "Of course, there were exceptions. There was one guy named Picky, who got that name because he was a master pickpocket. He could steal a man's socks right off his feet without him knowing. Believe me, Picky got us chased out of more than a few towns."

After a few months of this grueling existence, Bill returned home and finished high school. Next came stints as a deputy sheriff in the Tallulah, Louisiana, Sheriff's Department, followed by a hitch in the U.S. Army. Then he began a career in radio broadcasting at KTLD in Tallulah, which would last sixteen years. It was there that he fine-tuned his storytelling skills. He turned to writing in 1970, but it wouldn't be until 1979 that his first novel, *The Devil's Kiss,* was published. Thus began the full-time writing career of William W. Johnstone. He wrote horror (*The Uninvited*), thrillers (*The Last of the Dog Team*), even a romance novel or two. Then, in February 1983, *Out of the Ashes* was published. Searching for his missing family in the aftermath of a post-apocalyptic America, rebel mercenary and patriot Ben Raines is united with the civilians of the Resistance forces and moves to the forefront of a revolution for the nation's future.

Out of the Ashes was a smash. The series would continue for the next twenty years, winning Bill three generations of fans all over the world. The series was often imitated but never duplicated. "We all tried to copy the Ashes series," said one publishing executive, "but Bill's uncanny ability, both then and now, to predict in which direction the political winds were blowing brought a certain immediacy to the table no one else could capture." The Ashes series would end its run with more than thirty-four books and twenty million copies in print, making it one of the most successful men's action series in American book publishing. (The Ashes series also, Bill notes with a touch of pride, got him on the FBI's Watch List for its less than flattering portrayal of spineless politicians and the growing power of big government over our lives, among other things. In that respect, I often find myself saying, "Bill was years ahead of his time.")

Always steps ahead of the political curve, Bill's recent thrillers, written with myself, include *Vengeance Is Mine, Invasion USA, Border War, Jackknife, Remember the Alamo, Home Invasion, Phoenix Rising, The Blood of*

Patriots, The Bleeding Edge, and the upcoming *Suicide Mission.*

It is with the western, though, that Bill found his greatest success and propelled him onto both the *USA Today* and the *New York Times* bestseller lists.

Bill's western series include *The Mountain Man, Matt Jensen, the Last Mountain Man, Preacher, The Family Jensen, Luke Jensen, Bounty Hunter, Eagles, MacCallister* (an Eagles spin-off), *Sidewinders, The Brothers O'Brien, Sixkiller, Blood Bond, The Last Gunfighter,* and the upcoming new series *Flintlock* and *The Trail West.* May 2013 saw the hardcover western *Butch Cassidy, The Lost Years.*

"The Western," Bill says, "is one of the few true art forms that is one hundred percent American. I liken the Western as America's version of England's Arthurian legends, like the Knights of the Round Table, or Robin Hood and his Merry Men. Starting with the 1902 publication of *The Virginian* by Owen Wister, and followed by the greats like Zane Grey, Max Brand, Ernest Haycox, and of course Louis L'Amour, the Western has helped to shape the cultural landscape of America.

"I'm no goggle-eyed college academic, so

when my fans ask me why the Western is as popular now as it was a century ago, I don't offer a 200-page thesis. Instead, I can only offer this: The Western is honest. In this great country, which is suffering under the yoke of political correctness, the Western harks back to an era when justice was sure and swift. Steal a man's horse, rustle his cattle, rob a bank, a stagecoach, or a train, you were hunted down and fitted with a hangman's noose. One size fit all.

"Sure, we westerners are prone to a little embellishment and exaggeration and, I admit it, occasionally play a little fast and loose with the facts. But we do so for a very good reason — to enhance the enjoyment of readers.

"It was Owen Wister, in *The Virginian* who first coined the phrase *'When you call me that, smile.'* Legend has it that Wister actually heard those words spoken by a deputy sheriff in Medicine Bow, Wyoming, when another poker player called him a son-of-a-bitch.

"Did it really happen, or is it one of those myths that have passed down from one generation to the next? I honestly don't know. But there's a line in one of my favorite Westerns of all time, *The Man Who Shot Liberty Valance,* where the newspaper editor tells the young reporter, 'When the truth becomes legend, print the legend.'

"These are the words I live by."

The employees of Thorndike Press hope you have enjoyed this Large Print book. All our Thorndike, Wheeler, and Kennebec Large Print titles are designed for easy reading, and all our books are made to last. Other Thorndike Press Large Print books are available at your library, through selected bookstores, or directly from us.

For information about titles, please call:
(800) 223-1244

or visit our Web site at:
http://gale.cengage.com/thorndike

To share your comments, please write:
Publisher
Thorndike Press
10 Water St., Suite 310
Waterville, ME 04901